ANNALA
MEMOIRS OF
A MERMAID

ANNALA
MEMOIRS OF A MERMAID

ALANNA MURPHY

ISBN: 978-1-78324-082-1

Published by Wordzworth
www.wordzworth.com

CONTENTS

ONE

NOW

Fort Lauderdale, FL
August 2015

The sun was beating down on my face this morning, making it impossible to continue sleeping. Magic, the small black cat I found outside my apartment last night stood up and stretched beside me. I decided to get out of bed, make myself some tea, and start writing. I've kept journals throughout my time, but now I feel as if it is time to write more than just a few words in my journal. The time has come for me to write about what I know, and what I don't know for that matter.

I woke up in my new apartment in Fort Lauderdale, Florida. It's been a while since I've been back to this part of the world but it feels like home. Actually, everywhere I go feels like home. I'm not one to really miss a place too much. Rather, I often miss the people I've met along the way. Sometimes I wonder if I will ever see some of those people again. Many have long since left this earth. From time to time I think about where they are and why I am still here.

I'm back in the Sunshine State, near the ocean, where I belong. This is my home for the moment. I need time alone to get my thoughts together and figure out what it is that I need to be doing. I have found that time spent alone is often when you learn the most. The Universe seems to place everything you need right in front of you. And right now, a pen and paper are just about the only things I need.

TWO

WHAT I KNOW

My name is Annala and I am very different from anyone I have ever crossed paths with. To clarify that last statement, I am what most people call "a mermaid." I will try my best to explain who or what I am, though I know I will face difficulties because I barely know myself. I have been wandering the earth for thousands of years. I am not quite clear on a good number of things. I don't know exactly where I came from, how long I will live here on earth, or what my purpose is.

I don't need much to survive. All I really need is a little bit of sleep every once in a while, a good meal every now and then, air (no, I cannot breathe underwater) and good company when I can find it. I also love music. I don't know how old I am but I usually tell people I am in my 20's. Sometimes I tell people I am 24, sometimes 27, sometimes 20, and sometimes I just make them guess and tell them they are right. It depends on whom I am talking to. The truth is, I don't think it matters how old you are. I've met people of all different ages with various mindsets. Some of the older ones have yet to really learn anything of importance, while some of the youngest ones have wisdom beyond their years.

Time is a strange concept to me, for obvious reasons. I've been around for a long time and have had the opportunity to see a lot and speak with a good number of people. I like people and I think people tend to like me too. I think I am drawn to people because in many ways, I am one of them. As soon as I hit the shore, I no longer have a fin. I am able to walk and act just like any other normal human being. I am also able to speak with whomever I meet. I know there are these barriers that separate people called language. However, for whatever reason, I can speak with anyone. Communicating comes naturally for me. Because of this, I have been able to learn a lot about people and about human nature.

I have also spent a lot of time alone, traveling the oceans and different lands. This earth is an amazing place. The more I've seen, the more I wonder about it all. There is so much beauty, but there is also so much destruction. I have watched the earth change for both the better and the worse. But as far as we know, it's all we've got. Protecting this unbelievable planet is important. Luckily, humans are a powerful bunch. Humans have the potential to really create a heaven here on Earth. After all, people created the system that governs their lives today. I'd like to think people are constantly working to change the system for the better. I guess only time will tell, as it always does.

THREE

DISCOVERIES

South Pacific
~800 CE

It was a long time ago. I distinctly remember when I set eyes on a human being for the very first time. I had been living near an island in the South Pacific. There are a great many islands in the area that I had spent years exploring. The ocean was my home, but the small bodies of land always gave me a heightened sense of adventure. I loved washing ashore and feeling my fin turn into a pair of legs that I could use to explore the unexplored lands. There was always something new to see, whether it was a little crab moving along the shore or the changing colors of a setting sun. There weren't any troubles in my life, but I couldn't help but feel as if something was missing. There needed to be more to life than swimming aimlessly around the sea. I had no recollection of my past and I didn't know how long I had been wandering around the South Pacific. The truth was, although I had always been a curious and adventurous young girl, I was too nervous to venture out past what I knew. I wondered what else was out there, but I was content bathing in the lagoons I knew so well. I would spend my nights staring at the endless sky of stars, dreaming of whether or not I would ever come across another like me. How could it be that schools of fish, all alike would spend their days together, heading to where they were supposed to be? Or why is it that when a young dolphin entered this world, it had its mother show it the way? I felt lost and confused but I continued to live day by day.

It was on a cloudy, tired morning that everything I knew changed. I was admiring a shell I found on the shore of one of my favorite islands. The shell was round and smooth along the edges with a hole in the center. It fit perfectly around my pinky finger. I put it on and decided I would keep it. I was trying to stay warm since the sun was tucked behind big, grey clouds. I closed my eyes for a few seconds and when I opened them, I thought I was dreaming. Off in the distance I saw something I had never seen before moving toward my island. I didn't know what to make of it. I swam into deeper water and watched for hours as it came closer and closer. I now know that what I was watching was a boat full of people, but at the time, I had never seen such a thing. I was uneasy. I was scared. I was excited. But the moment that really changed my life forever was the moment I saw what was in the boat. Creatures that almost identically resembled me were heading my way! I kept my distance for a while. Months went by and I watched from the sea. I became more and more curious about the humans. I realized pretty quickly that they were a different breed. They were a land animal. They entered the ocean regularly but only for short periods of time to bathe or catch fish. They had also brought with them plants and animals that I had never seen before. Dogs, pigs and chickens now inhabited the island I had known so well. Bananas, taro, coconut and sugarcane were all brought to the island as well. In a sense, I felt possessive over the island I had once called my home. I didn't like seeing it all change so quickly. But I also remained curious about these people. Where did they come from? What else was out there?

On one brave night I decided to venture close to shore. The people had all gone to sleep. I slowly made my way to shore and started to walk around quietly. The people had built little huts that they slept in and I crept around them trying not to make too much noise.

As I walked around the corner of a hut, I tripped on a branch. A dog started barking frantically. I panicked. As I turned to run away, I saw a young woman staring straight at me.

I stared back, shocked, unable to move my feet. As I looked into her eyes, I felt as if I knew her. I sensed her kindness. She opened her mouth to say something and I panicked. I turned and started to run toward the sea. She followed. Finally, she screamed, "stop, please!" She was speaking to me and I understood her.

I stopped and stared again. She had caught up to me. We were standing beneath a coconut tree with a waxing gibbous moon above our heads. She reached out her hand and touched my arm. She asked who I was. I didn't answer. She asked where I came from. Again, I didn't answer. She pointed to herself to introduce herself as Maka Koa. For the first time, ever, I spoke to another human being. I told her my name was Annala. And so it was.

She looked at me curiously, with a bold confidence. She smiled. I turned from her and quickly approached the calm sea. From this point on, my life would never be the same.

FOUR

TEA PLANTATIONS, SWORD SWALLOWERS & THE FORTUNE TELLER

"China's Golden Age"

~960-1279 CE

From my first real human interaction with Maka Koa, I couldn't help but wonder what else was out there, and there was only one way to find out. I headed northwest. I arrived in China just before sunrise on a warm summer day. I didn't know where I was or what to expect from this new land. I washed ashore in Mingzhou, now known as Ningbo. It was a seaport town and it was evident that it was a center for maritime trade. While the sun came up, I wandered into town and as the sky brightened, so did Mingzhou. Merchants and seamen were hard at work packing up silk, porcelain, tea and medicines that would be shipped to Japan, Shilla and Southeast Asia. I tried to lay low, but I didn't exactly blend in with my bare feet and the small cloth wrapped around my body as a dress. A few men stared at me but I tried to continue walking without making any eye contact. Luckily, nobody bothered me. I wandered freely throughout the city, taking in everything I could. And so I spent days, weeks, months exploring the city by day and returning to the sea at night.

One rainy afternoon, I took a route in town I had yet to explore. I found myself lost in a Muslim ghetto. With time, I had observed the fact that there was a large Muslim community amongst the more prominent Chinese community. This was the first, but certainly not the last, time I observed the separation of people based on religion or ethnicity. The Muslim ghettos were poorer than the local Chinese community. However, everyone seemed to live in peace overall. The Muslims were free to practice their religion and some Muslim men even married Chinese women. I must have looked lost when a young Chinese girl approached me. While I had spent quite a bit of time exploring Mingzhou, I had very few interactions with people. This would be the first conversation I would hold with someone since my meeting with Maka Koa.

The Chinese girl asked me if I needed help. I looked at her, hesitantly, and asked if she could point me in the direction of the sea. She did, but not before she asked me my name. "Annala" I told her. She smiled and told me she had seen me in town once before. She asked me where I was going and I shrugged, not really knowing myself. She laughed a little bit and asked if I was looking for work. She told me that her family owned a farm not too far from town. She would be accompanying her husband to the farm early tomorrow morning. She told me her family could use the help on their tea plantation.

And so I went, with my first real friend. Her name was Li. Li's husband, Amr, was a Muslim merchant. He did a good business selling her family's tea.

Li's family welcomed me with open arms. They housed me, clothed me, fed me and gave me more tea than I could drink. I worked hard on their farm and I loved every minute of it. Not only was farming new to me, but so was tea. The concept of drinking anything but water struck me as unusual at first, but tea was something special. I loved all the different varieties and I grew interested in learning about the medicinal benefits of various kinds. Tea would become a part of my life from here on out. What I loved most about Li's family was how open-minded they were. They kindly accepted Amr as a part of the family despite their religious differences. Amr was an amazing man as well. For the first time, I felt as if I had a family. I spoke to Li and Amr about religion, money, travel, love and so much more. I was learning so much about people and the society they lived in. There were so many rules in place and many of them were hard for me to understand at first. Money was something I had never been exposed to before arriving in China. Food was always plentiful for me as I could live off seaweed itself to survive. However, trying all kinds of different recipes that people cooked up was definitely a treat. Of course it made sense that people needed some sort of currency to trade in exchange for goods. Li's family lived off of the basics, but any extra money they could get was helpful. Religion was also a very interesting concept to me. I was able to learn about both Neo-Confucianism as well as Islam. I liked them both. It seemed that at the end of the day, both religions emphasized being a good person. Li's family told me that many people got caught up in the technicalities of religion and failed to realize that love is all that matters. It wasn't hard to see that Li's family had a deep love for each other, for nature, for their work, for other people and for life itself. I really admired how madly in love Amr and Li were as well. I felt at peace with them.

However, as time went on, I started to get anxious and curious again. Things were changing in China and I felt the need to continue my journey. I was sad to say goodbye to these people that had become a family to me, but it was time for me to go. I headed in the direction of Lin'an.

I took my time venturing to Lin'an (now known as Hangzhou), stopping in other towns and returning to the sea at times. I stayed mostly along the coast as I headed North from Mingzhou, but I would occasionally explore some inland areas as well. The sea was still my home and I felt safe when in the vicinity of the ocean. It was a place of refuge for me.

When I arrived in Lin'an, it was hard not to be overwhelmed. Lin'an was the capital and it was one of the biggest cities in the world. The streets were bustling with acrobats, puppeteers, snake charmers, fortunetellers, actors, sword swallowers and storytellers. Life was much different in Lin'an than it was on the countryside but I liked it. The excitement of being in such a city ignited a flame inside of me. I was ready for whatever life had in store for me next.

I took a job working in a tavern, serving hot wine and food to guests that came in. There were often large parties, drinking and celebrating some sort of occasion. I enjoyed the job, as I was able to observe all the different people that came in.

One night, I was serving hot wine to a large group of people. They were drinking quite a bit and started speaking with me. One middle-aged lady took a liking to me. She was very friendly and kept commenting on how beautiful I was. She invited me out with her and her friends the following night. I could tell she was wealthy from the way she spoke about the Antique Collectors' club and the refined Music Society. She seemed to have a passion for luxurious living.

So Hua became my friend. She invited me everywhere with her. We frequented the markets, sipped tea at the finest tea houses and soaked our bodies in the hot baths multiple times a month. Hua acted as a friend, but also as a guardian. She took me under her wing and insisted on treating me to only first-class amenities. With her I became one of the urban elite. Hua bought me expensive clothing and jewelry. She often tried to convince me to remove the shell ring from my pinky because it wasn't "stylish." But that shell ring felt as if it was a part of me, a part of my past, so I left it on.

My absolute favorite part of the city was the entertainment quarters of Kaifeng. I would spend hours aimlessly walking around, stopping often to listen to a storyteller or watching the snake charmers. There were two men who I often watched as they performed on the street together. The two of them were sword swallowers and they knew how to put on a good show. Enthralled, I would frequent their street to watch them perform. They would notice me and smile and I always gave them money when I could. I didn't know them, but I liked them.

Hua and I got along great. She would gossip to me for hours and I always listened. She was a good person, but she focused on "things." She was eager to buy anything new and stylish, while I didn't care much for anything I didn't really need. I was just as happy to give any extra money to the street performers or the beggars. However, I did love my tea. Tea was a luxury I wasn't willing to give up.

I learned a lot from Hua. She opened my eyes to what money can buy. It can certainly buy you a good time, but it didn't take me long to learn that it wouldn't buy someone happiness. Overall, Hua was a happy woman, but many of her friends were not. I saw women in competition over who had the more expensive necklace or whose husband made more money. Hua never married. She thought men were dirty and treacherous. She had many strong opinions and I admired that about her. Despite the fact that she cared about status and societal standings, she held her ground on certain beliefs, one of which was her dismissal of foot binding. Women started binding their feet in China at this time in order to display status. Wealthy women who didn't need their feet for work would have them bound. Hua thought this "beauty symbol" was an evil practice and she refused to be a part of it. She was witty and charming and I was happy to have met her. While I loved life in the city, I started to miss the simplicity of the countryside. It had been awhile since I had woken up early to watch the sunrise. Life in Lin'an was fast-paced and exciting but I started to get an urge again. Was there something else for me to see or do?

On an overcast afternoon in the entertainment quarters of Kaifeng, a fortuneteller lured me in. Intrigued by what she might have to say, I stopped. She was old and I could tell she had been doing this for a while. She looked at me, up and down, before revealing any of her knowledge. She finally spoke, in an old, cracking voice…

"My dear, you are very unique and it is not easy for me to read you, but I can tell you one thing. The time has come. The Mongols will soon invade. You have a way out. Take it now."

She continued to look at me. She cracked a smile and then motioned for me to leave. I looked at her, wondering, skeptical, and then I walked away. She got me thinking. She might have been a crazy old lady, but I took it as a sign. It was time for me to leave.

FIVE

DREAMS

Australia
~1300s CE

From the time I left China, I took to the ocean. I swam for a long time. I felt something pulling me in a direction. I was heading south. I spent day after day swimming toward something big. There were countless bodies of land I encountered, but something told me to keep going. I listened. Eventually I reached the large landmass known as Australia.

When I arrived at this land it felt right. I felt my fin turn into feet for the first time in awhile and I was ready to put my feet to use. Australia was still unexplored at this time. As I spent months exploring Australia's coasts, I came across Aborigines that had settled in communities along the shore. I stayed far enough away to observe without being noticed. I quickly realized that this land was much more remote than the areas of China I had been living in. The people lived in a very different manner. The Aborigines migrated with the seasons. When it came to collecting food, women and men had defined tasks. The women would gather plants and small animals such as lizards and turtles, while the men hunted larger animals such as wallabies and kangaroos. Even though these people lived with much "less" than what I had gotten used to in Lin'an, they seemed to be happy. The earth provided them with everything they needed. Rather than build large cities and settle in one location, the Aborigines lived a hunter-gatherer lifestyle and lived off of the natural resources provided to them.

For a while I stayed along the northern coast. I explored the land, but I also explored the ocean along the northeast. The Great Barrier Reef was unlike any other coral reef I had seen. Hundreds of species of coral and over a thousand species of fish could keep me fascinated for a lifetime. As always, I felt comfortable and safe in the ocean. But the time came for me to hit the land and move away from "safety."

I decided to venture inland and I quickly fell in love with the land. I appreciated the variety of natural beauty Earth's landmasses had to offer. From the north I experienced the tropical side of Australia. Venturing through thick, mysterious rainforests, it was often scary making my way through the trees alone. At night there were loud noises of nature and often when I slept, I started to have detailed dreams. In the past, I didn't always remember my dreams. However, lately, they started to appear vividly and frequently. I came across snakes, giant insects, and tons of other little creatures I had never seen before. Bright and colorful birds flew effortlessly through the trees, kangaroos and possums scurried through shrubs, and the variety of plants and animals left me fascinated. I grew to adore the little tree kangaroos that would leap from one tree to another, often stopping to stare at me curiously and apprehensively. Every single day I found myself more amazed and inspired by the earth. How could there be such a variety of different species? There were so many different kinds of birds, frogs, lizards and insects. They all seemed to have some sort of purpose. They lived their lives, knowing what to do and how to do it. Even people across the different areas I had visited resembled each other but still had their differences in appearance and behavior. What a wild world this was. My body grew strong. My legs gained muscle from climbing mountains and navigating through rough terrain. I started to learn both about the land, as well as about myself. Through experiences with certain bodies of water, I realized my feet only turned into a fin when exposed to salt water, rather than fresh water. I had experienced this before, but it was made evident on my journey through Australia when I bathed in rivers and falls, never to see my fin emerge. I guess the salty sea was the secret elixir to turn me back into a mermaid. That meant that the more inland I ventured, the more human I became. The towering mountains, alluring falls, and lush rainforests became my playground. I loved this land.

I went from the dense, green forests to vast grasslands. The lands shifted and changed before my eyes. The air and temperature changed as I moved further inland. It was all so new and exciting. Eventually I reached desert lands. The colorful sands, exquisite gorges and rocks, and endless arid terrain left me hypnotized. I didn't know how long I had been traveling for and I started to panic. What if I never found my way back to the sea? What if I encountered wild animals or people that wanted to kill or eat me? I didn't know what had come over me but I started to worry myself sick. I had never been this far from the ocean on my own. My dreams started to haunt me. I dreamed of being lost, running away from something trying to catch me, and being unable to find water. My waking worries were starting to manifest themselves in my sleep. I also had many dreams about tidal waves. What did all this mean? Where was I going?

As I continued to wander, deeper and deeper into this foreign land, my skin drying and throat aching, I started to lose hope. Maybe I should turn around and try to find my way back the way I came... Just when I thought all was lost, I spotted a group of people in the distance. Nervous, but left with no other option, I headed in their direction. I reached them at nightfall. As I approached, I noticed they seemed to be involved in some sort of ceremony. They were dancing and chanting and seemingly summoning something. I got closer. One older man noticed me and stopped what he was doing. Others followed. In a matter of seconds, the entire group was staring at me, dumbfounded.

The older man said something that I couldn't make out. He started to laugh and clap. I didn't know what to do. He looked at me and slowly, I moved in closer and closer. As I came in contact with the group, they stepped aside so that I could approach the old man who was the furthest away from me. When I reached him, he touched my arm, stared at me a little while longer and then motioned for me to follow him. I did.

We went into a sort of rock dwelling. There was an old woman inside. She had colored rocks and clays beside her and I noticed drawings on the walls of the cave. She looked at me and asked who I was. "Annala," I told her. She looked at the man and said, "she understands." The man nodded and then asked me where I came from. "From the sea," I murmured. The two of them looked at each other and I saw a slight smile cross each of their faces.

For the next few days, they fed me, gave me water, provided me with clothing and made sure I was safe. The old man and woman only let me interact with certain individuals. They treated me well and I soon came to realize they believed I was some sort of heavenly being sent to deliver a message to them.

They started talking to me about "Dreamtime," which connected their past, present and future. They taught me about the mythic being that created the land and had since withdrawn to the spiritual world. They told me the spiritual beings usually sent them messages through dreams. Different members of the tribe would visit me in the cave and ask me all kinds of questions. They wanted to know who I was, where I came from, what I had seen, what I came to tell them and so much more. It was a little overwhelming at first but I started to get used to it and even enjoy it. I told them stories about the ocean and all the creatures of the sea. I told them about the South Pacific and Maka Koa. I told them about China and tea and all the luxuries I enjoyed in Lin'an. They couldn't believe everything I was telling them. They truly thought I was a goddess and it was nice to be so revered.

As they told me about Dreamtime and some of their rituals, I revealed to them that I had been having nightmares during my journeys in this land. There was one particular dream that recurred over and over. It was always slightly different, but with the same feel overall. In the most recent dream, I was at a beach with a large, sandy cliff overlooking the sea. The waves were rough but people were still swimming in the ocean. I was one of the people in the ocean. As I swam out, the current became more powerful and the waves grew larger. I struggled against the wind and the waves as they crashed over me. I kept trying to avoid the pounding waves by going under them, but every time I came up for air, there was another wave ready to crash down on me. I would always awake, out of breath, before anything else would happen. Usually I am very comfortable in the ocean. It is my home. But this was a different feeling that I couldn't explain.

The Dreamtime leaders tried to analyze what was going on in my head. They believed I was one of the spiritual creators and they thought my dreams were a message important to mankind. They took my dream as a sign that a great change would occur, for them and for me as well. It would be a difficult and overwhelming change, but an inevitable one. I listened intently and tried to make sense of it all. Could it be that I was some sort of spiritual being connected to the gods like they thought? As time went on, I became much more immersed in the culture of these desert Aborigines. They showed me how to find water holes (another tactic they learned through dreaming) and identified various plants and their uses. They hunted, gathered, and taught me how to use fires, not only to keep warm, but also to manage the plants and animals in the land. They told me that fire had its own dreaming stories as well.

I partook in various spiritual ceremonies with them and they made me cloaks from possum and wallaby skins. I became a focus of the ceremonies and I found that people started to come to me for answers to questions I rarely knew the answers to. They would ask me when rain would come or whether pregnant members would have a boy or a girl. Of course I never knew but I tried my best to provide some sort of answer. I followed this group of people as they moved from place to place and made use of the natural resources provided.

What I really loved most about these people was their practicality. They had no accumulation of goods. They kept only what they had a use for, earning respect from each other through ritual knowledge rather than wealth. Living within their means, these people utilized everything the earth provided them with, and overall, they were happy. I was also happy. I felt safe with them, but I never fully felt at home. I was itching for the sea. I knew these people would be hesitant to let me leave and I didn't want to risk it. I planned to leave late one night. I fell asleep early in the evening only to be woken up around midnight by another tidal wave dream. It was earlier than I planned to leave, but I couldn't fall back asleep. I escaped into the night.

SIX

THE WRITER

The Mali Empire
~1350 CE

The funny thing about traveling is that you never really know what time it is. For me, I mean that in terms of days, years, decades, and centuries. Time is a strange concept. All these things are happening all around us. So much is happening all at once, but as an individual, you get caught in a moment. I often think about past moments, memories, and their significance to me. Other times I think about future moments, things I know are bound to happen, my current path leading up to them, only to one day make them memories. Our existence consists of memories. Some are of greater importance than others, and these memories make us who we are.

I continued journeying through the outback for a while before I reached the sea again. I don't know how long I had been traveling through the land, continuing to observe people, animals and nature that continued to blow my mind. Every little area seemed to hold a new variety of species. I saw kangaroos,

koalas, crocodiles, so many kinds of birds, snakes, frogs, and such
vast landscapes. It was all so incredible.

I finally got to the ocean and it was such an amazing feeling.
Feeling my fin for the first time again was indescribable. I felt free
and at ease. I took my time traveling through the ocean. I swam
far and deep, appreciating the beauty of the various fish and other
sea life. There was a pod of dolphins that accompanied me on my
journey for a while. I felt as if they were guiding me along the blue
seas, going in the direction of something new and bright. I felt a
deep connection to these majestic creatures that were so playful
and alive. I could tell they liked me and I enjoyed their company.
Tasting seaweed again ignited old memories. I had been eating
much more meat with the Aborigines than I was used to, and getting back on my seaweed diet was refreshing. Life was simple again.

Eventually, I reached my new destination, West Africa. My
first stop was the capital of the Mali Empire. It was clear that the

people here lived a much different lifestyle than the Australian Aborigines. Grand palaces, mosques, gold, slaves, army men, kings, and scholars all made for an interesting place. When I arrived, Mansa Suleyman was in charge. People told me stories about the previous king, Musa Keita I, the powerful brother of Suleyman. The stories about Musa Keita were astonishing. Musa was a devout Muslim. Apparently, he became well known across the Middle East and North Africa when he made his pilgrimage to Mecca. Along his journeys, Musa and his 60,000 men, along with his numerous camels and horses, carried thousands of pounds of gold, generously distributing gold to the poor along the way. Musa built mosques and madrasas in Timbuktu and Gao. He also built the Sankore Madrasah, which was staffed with mathematicians, jurists and astronomers. Someone recently told me that Musa Keita was the wealthiest man to have ever lived. I believe it.

During my journeys in West Africa, I encountered all types of people. I interacted with slave girls, army men, religious fanatics, and children of the sultan. One of the most interesting men I met during my time in Mali was an author named Ibn. Ibn traveled extensively through Africa, Eastern Europe, the Middle East, South and Central Asia, and China. He had endless tales about sailing to the Swahili Coast, marrying into a royal family in the Maldive Islands, being attacked by pirates after his ship almost sunk while embarking from Sri Lanka, and the Black Death turning cities into ghost towns. I could sit and listen to him speak for what seemed like forever. I bombarded him with questions, being curious about the enchanting lands he traveled to. He told me about leaving home and how difficult it had been. However, many pious men told him that foreign travel was his destiny. I listened intently, thinking about my own destiny. Was I destined for something? It seemed travel was in my cards as well.

Ibn was religious but he was open-minded. While he disapproved of the fact that the female slaves and servants exposed more of their bodies than a Muslim woman should be allowed, his travels had opened his mind to various lifestyles. While living in Mali, I made sure to keep myself covered as to not draw too much attention to myself. It felt unnatural to be so layered in clothing, but this was the way of the land. Ibn and I traveled by camel to Timbuktu. Timbuktu would later become one of the most important cities in the region, but at the time, it was fairly small. One of the most memorable days of our journey was the day we encountered a hippopotamus. Ibn had seen a good number of creatures in his travels, as had I. However, many feared this aggressive water animal. Local boatmen would hunt the hippos using lances with strong cords attached. These were scary creatures, mostly because of how aggressive they were. Even the crocodiles and venomous snakes in Australia were less frightening than the hippos. However, though these hippos seemed so scary, I found it interesting when I learned that hippos are actually vegetarians. The only reason they are so aggressive is to protect their young. When a creature feels threatened or feels as if their family or lifestyle might be threatened, they will do anything for protection. This holds true for humans and every other creature of the earth.

One of the greatest influences Ibn had on me was writing. Ibn was an author, constantly taking note of the happenings of his journeys. As Ibn spent many a night writing in his journal, I started to do the same.

I told Ibn some of my stories but I tried not to reveal too much. Luckily for me, Ibn was more of a talker than a listener and he had more than enough to talk about. We liked each other and after a short amount of time in Timbuktu, we traveled down the Niger River by canoe to Gao.

One dark night, Ibn was chatting away to me about the silk and porcelain of China. He then started telling me about the Taoist monk he visited in a cave in Quanzhou. His story was interesting but I was tired after a long day. As I started to close my eyes, Ibn reached out his arm and touched my leg. I quickly awoke, my heart beating fast. He was making a pass at me and I didn't know how to react. This was all so new to me. I liked Ibn but this wasn't something I wanted. I jolted back awkwardly. As he tried to pursue me, I got up and walked away.

Maybe that was the wrong way to react but I didn't know what else to do. Ibn had told me about his many other wives he had acquired during his journey, and I didn't feel good about being one of his women. After observing many relationships between men and women in the various parts of the world I had traveled to, I had made up my mind that I wanted to find love. I didn't love Ibn and he didn't love me. Not in that way at least.

I spent more time in Gao. It was there that I met a young servant girl named Inari. Influenced by an empire ruled by gold, Inari spent her days dreaming about acquiring the finest silk dresses, living in a palace and dousing herself in gold dust. This was all she talked about. While she was caught up in these material objects, she had a good heart. She was emotional, sensitive and she always seemed to be preoccupied in her thoughts. She liked talking to me, not only because I listened, but also because I offered sound advice. I told her these riches would not make her any happier. I told her about my experiences with people who lived off the land, with no care for anything that wasn't useful. She listened and seemed to understand, but I could never fully get through to her. She lived in a world governed by "status" and that was all she knew or cared about. I wanted her to know that there was so much more to this beautiful planet. She admired me and I hope that some of what I told her sank in. She liked playing with the shell I wore on my pinky finger. I told her about the day I found it. I told her about the turquoise waters, patterned shells and playful dolphins of the oceans. I told her that watching the show painted by the sky in the morning would give her more joy than a gold bar. I told her that people needed to work together. I had just started to learn all these lessons myself. Traveling through West Africa gave me even more insight into human nature than I had learned before my arrival to this land. The more "wealth" one acquired, the more powerful he became. This was great when the one in power used it to do good things. However, I would quickly learn that not everyone with power and wealth was so giving. Many of the wealthiest people were also the greediest. People always want more.

I hope Inari grew to acquire all the riches she dreamed of, though I know it wouldn't have changed her state of mind.

SEVEN

THE MAN I ALMOST REVEALED MY SECRET TO

Italy
The Renaissance
~1450 CE

A s I explored and learned about new lands and ways of life, I grew more eager to travel and more confident in my ability to do so. I discovered I had been growing more curious as my journey continued. I had already seen so much and I became convinced that there was so much more to see and do.

I followed the wind, the sea and my heart to Italy. It was mid-1400's and a great change was occurring. I could *feel* it.

I found myself in Florence. It was here that I met the man I almost revealed my secret to. His name was Cosimo.

Cosimo was more than just charming; he was intelligent, aware, and filled with life. Upon meeting him, I trusted him and felt as if I knew him. The way he looked at me was unlike anything I had experienced. He wanted to see me all the time and I wanted to see him too. Cosimo was a scholar. He studied history, poetry and philosophy. Art and music were of the utmost importance to him. I felt comfortable with him and I grew more comfortable with myself as well.

I remember the first time I "met" Cosimo. I write, "met" because I often think that I have known him throughout existence. Yes, there is an initial "meeting point" on this earth, however, I feel as if before and after we exist on this planet, there are certain, significant individuals who travel with us through time and space. It is important to recognize who those individuals are because those are the ones that will guide you along on your path and help you find exactly what it is that you need to be doing while living on Earth. So, I "met" Cosimo in Florence on a bright day while sitting outside. I was writing in my journal, collecting some of my thoughts from my past experiences, feeling excited about what my life had in store for me next. I saw a man in the distance walking my way. For some reason he interested me. He was attractive and had an air about him that drew me toward him. I watched him for a couple of minutes and then returned to my writings. I looked up again and he was much closer to me now, still heading in my direction, but now he was looking at me. We were looking at each other. I smiled, a shy but sincere smile. He smiled back.

Cosimo approached me, smiling all the while, and asked me my name. After introducing ourselves to each other, he asked me what I was doing. I told him I was just putting some thoughts down on paper. He then asked me about the shell I wore on my finger. I told him I found it on the beach. He asked to see it so I took it off and handed it to him. He spun it around, admiring it, and told me it was unique and he liked it. I saw a twinkle in his eye as he looked at me. He was nervous but confident at the same time. He invited me to have dinner and wine with him that evening. I agreed.

I was anxious about meeting Cosimo that night. Though I was excited, I was also timid. I guess it was sort of a date and I had never done this before. However, when we began talking, everything felt right. Conversation flowed and he was so interested in me. Throughout my time, I had encountered countless people who loved to talk. They often had plenty of interesting things to talk about and I am much more of a listener anyways. I was always shy and I would prefer to listen to someone rather than speak about myself. But with Cosimo, he seemed to be genuinely interested in what I had to say. So I told him stories. I told him about certain people I had met and about some of my travels, mostly throughout Italy. I told him some of my ideas about human nature and about the world. I impressed him, and it was a good feeling.

We spent many days and nights together, talking and getting to know each other. We became the best of friends. Art, architecture, science and philosophy kept us engaged in conversations for hours on end. He knew so much about art and the current trends that were starting to ignite in the art world. He knew all about different technicalities, while I offered a more abstract view. We complimented each other quite well in our ideas. I also became friends with many of his friends. His friends included artists, poets and scientists. They were all so interesting to me. They all had a curiosity about this world and an urge to uncover secrets to our existence.

As time went on and Cosimo and I became closer and closer, I could tell he liked me more than just as a friend. While I was comfortable and confident in his presence, I was still shy solely because I had never experienced certain things.

Late one night, after a good amount of wine and a conversation that was starting to die down, Cosimo started to work up his courage. I distinctly remember sitting outside with him, looking up at the stars, when he took my face in his hands, looking at me intently and with passion, and then leaned in to kiss me. My heart racing in a manner I had never experienced, I went with it. It was scary and awkward, but I liked it. I told him I had never kissed someone before. He smiled and kissed me again. We were both happy. We were good friends, but this was something new. It marked a new era in my life.

Cosimo became my first boyfriend. It was a fun and adolescent relationship. He could sense my innocence and I could tell he never wanted to do anything that would make me uncomfortable. He tried venturing further into our physical relationship a few times, but it was all still so new to me, and I never knew what to do or how to react. I didn't know much about sex, and I didn't feel ready. He always respected what I wanted to do. While sex was thought of as a sort of sin in Italy at this time, sexuality was becoming less of an "evil." It would take me much more time to become comfortable as a woman and become comfortable being viewed as "sexy."

During the Renaissance, ideas were spreading like wildfire. The invention of printing advanced new concepts and brought back to light the ideas of ancient Greek and Roman thinkers. People started questioning the Church. Transformations were beginning to occur in society and there was a gradual shift in the way people thought. Cosimo had always been a religious skeptic, often criticizing perceived corruptions of the Church. I liked living in this society that had so many free thinkers. People were skeptical about the current systems, curious about life and working toward new inventions that would change the world.

Another luxury (besides tea) I grew to love was wine. The right amount always intoxicated me in the best way possible. It was customary for Cosimo and I to indulge in wine regularly. One evening, while Cosimo and I sipped on the fine beverage, I found myself caught up in a profound, romantic conversation with this man I cared for deeply. He started talking about our future. He started inferring he wanted to spend the rest of his life with me. While I was always open and honest with Cosimo, there was much about my past I didn't reveal to him. How could I? I was supposedly 23, living in Italy, as a normal human being.

I could tell that he was trying to test out the waters to see what was going on in my head. He was looking for a reaction out of me, and the reaction I gave him wasn't what he was hoping for. I told him things weren't as simple as he thought. He looked confused and frustrated as I fought the urge to tell him *everything*.

This was our first "fight" and I hated it. I was going through so much inner turmoil and I truly didn't know what to do. I broke it down into two options:

1   I could tell him everything. By telling him everything, I would face my unknown future with him by my side. We could figure out what to do together. However, sooner or later he would grow old and I would continue to stay the way I've stayed for the past thousand years. We would likely have to move locations from time to time so people wouldn't suspect anything. I truly felt as if he was my best friend and leaving him would be difficult, however, I still had some doubts about our relationship and still had a wild curiosity and urge to move on to whatever else was awaiting me in the world.

2   I could refrain from telling him my secret, but be honest about my conflicted feelings regardless. I could tell him that despite the fact that I cared for him deeply, I was still too curious about the world to settle down, at least not yet. I felt as if there was so much more to explore and discover, and it wasn't time for me to stay in one place with one person. This would be extremely difficult to do as well.

Neither option would be easy, but after much consideration, I knew what I had to do. Sometimes it is difficult to listen to your own intuition, especially when you have other people nudging you to go along with *their* plan, but as soon as you dig deep inside and follow your heart, things work out the way they should.

Things had been different between Cosimo and I after that discussion. I had been at war with myself over the whole thing and he started questioning my feelings for him.

After a little bit of time, I finally decided I had to talk to him. We hadn't really discussed anything since he brought it up the first time, though we could both sense it was on each of our minds.

I asked if he wanted to take a stroll with me, something we often did. Though this time, we both knew it would be different.

We found a green area to sit and I started to tell him a little bit of what was going through my mind. I told him I wasn't ready to settle down like most girls were. I told him I had a strong desire to travel and see the world, and there were so many other people I had yet to meet and places I had yet to see. I wanted him to know that he was my best friend and I had never had such a connection with anyone before in my life, but it was coming time for me to leave once again. While he was upset and hurt, he understood. This is what I loved most about him. He never angered at me and he was always so understanding and patient with me. He knew I wasn't like many of the other girls who strived only to get married and have children. I had too many other things I wanted to do with my life first, and I think that is why he fell for me. I know it was difficult for him to let go of me because it was difficult for me to let go of him.

In my final weeks in Florence, we met up a couple of times. We were friendly and had some basic conversations, but the dynamic between us had changed. It was sad but inevitable. It was time for me to move on. I never saw Cosimo after that and I couldn't even tell you what ever happened to him, however, I am confident he lived a fulfilled life. Maybe one day we will "meet" again.

EIGHT

CONTROL

Spain
1492-1502

L eaving Italy was hard. Not only because of Cosimo, but also because of all the open-minded people I had connected with. I felt a strong, positive energy during my time there. Now I had a strange feeling as I ventured on. Was I right in my decision of leaving Cosimo behind? I was feeling solemn and unsure.

I traveled along the shores of Italy and France, sometimes venturing off and exploring some nearby islands before I finally reached Spain. My spirits were lifted as I continued my journey and continued to see how much more was out there. There were always interesting people to talk to and amazing nature to explore. It was late 1400's when I decided to settle in Spain. King Ferdinand and Queen Isabella ruled the land. I reached Spain at the height of much religious tension. In my first year living in Spain, Ferdinand and Isabella decided that any Jewish person who refused to convert to Christianity would be expelled from Spain.

I took a job in Seville as a domestic servant. I lived with a wealthy family. I worked hard cooking, washing and attending to the heads of the household. Beatriz, the lady of the house, was always very nice to me. I think she liked me because I did what I needed to and rarely involved myself in much else. I kept my mouth shut as she gossiped to me and made sure I was clear on all of her very strong opinions.

In my free time I would spend my days down by the river. It was here that I found refuge from the menial tasks of the week. I would walk alone through the greenery and bathe myself in the fresh waters of the flowing river. I worked so often that I didn't have much time to meet anyone new or explore as much as I wanted. I found myself feeling lonely amongst the women in my house. All they ever seemed to care about was their money, their beauty or the local gossip. I tried to care about what they spoke of, but I couldn't force myself to have any interest at all. Despite the fact they treated me well, I couldn't connect with them.

It took me some time before I made my first real friend. Her name was Ana. I met her on a day when I had some free time by the river. Ana was a young Jewish girl who had recently converted under the new law. She was friendly and upbeat. We became close as we spent many afternoons together, relaxing under the sun, speaking about things that always felt important. She told me about all the pressure she felt because of the fact that she was born Jewish. Life was harder for her because she wasn't accepted here. I couldn't understand why anyone cared what religion anyone else practiced. Wasn't the point of religion acceptance and being a good person? The fact that anyone would try to control someone else's beliefs is a concept I still cannot wrap my head around.

One afternoon, Beatriz asked to speak with me in private. I followed her into her lavish room where she sat me down and told me that she saw something that really bothered her. She noticed I had befriended Ana and she told me that her own reputation could be jeopardized by the fact that I was hanging out with a Jewish girl. I stared at Beatriz puzzled as she expressed such concern over my newfound friendship. I told Beatriz that Ana's family had converted, as if that made them better people. But Beatriz was still skeptical about the sincerity of their conversion. She said she didn't trust them and her friends agreed. I tried to understand why Beatriz cared about their religion. I had witnessed first hand that religion didn't have anything to do with how good of a person anyone was. Beatriz told me she would feel much better if I didn't spend time with Ana.

I was frustrated and upset. I couldn't exactly tell Beatriz how I felt. Even if I tried, she wouldn't understand. I also didn't know what to say to Ana. How could I tell Ana that Beatriz was *embarrassed* by me spending time with her. None of it made sense. Should I even attempt to tell Ana? I wouldn't even know how to go about it without hurting her feelings. But I couldn't exactly refuse to listen to Beatriz either. She provided me with a home and went over and beyond to make sure I had everything I needed.

Beatriz acted as a parent to me. In many ways she treated me like her own daughter. Her girls were always very nice to me as well. Even though I served them, Beatriz would buy me little things and included me in family events. In many ways she was a strong woman. However, in other ways she was very weak. Despite her "fighter" personality, she suffered from paranoia and constantly worried about what others thought of her. She wanted to be viewed as wealthy, generous, fun and intelligent; all of which she was. But from my perspective, the "show" was more important than the true connections she failed to make. It took me many years before I felt as if I began to figure her out. People are complicated beings. Especially when placed in a society governed by status. Beatriz also suffered from depression. I spent many nights trying to console her as she wept. I didn't understand why she cared so much about what other people thought and I didn't understand why she worried so much. It was ironic because she always spoke about having faith and praying to god, but I felt as if I had more trust in the Universe than this supposedly religious woman. I guess I just didn't understand her, and I am sure she didn't understand me.

After my discussion with Beatriz, I debated what to do about Ana. I knew that Ana was the only person present in my life at the moment who I could truly open up to. It would be hard to just cut her out. I decided I would talk to her and let her know about what Beatriz had said and what was going through my mind.

When I saw Ana next, she told me she had news for me. I let her speak first. She told me her family would be moving. It was too hard for them to live here amongst people that were always suspicious that they weren't true to the Christian faith. They felt like outsiders. I understood why. I decided not to mention anything about my discussion with Beatriz. What was the point?

I was feeling sad and angry. People can be so simple-minded and selfish.

I continued to work for Beatriz for many years. I stayed busy and worked hard. However, I often felt lonely, even in the presence of people that cared about me. It is funny how easy it is to get caught up in whatever life you are living. Even though I wasn't truly happy, the security I felt there made it easy to stay. I have found that a lot of people get caught up in life, forgetting about the dreams of their youth. Work, family, and the feeling of security hold many people back from passionately living. Days, months, and years passed me by before I got up the courage to continue on. There were times I often felt regretful about wasting so much time there, but I am glad I didn't spend more time than I did. I learned a lot about human nature as I lived with Beatriz and her family. There is no reason to fret over lost time. Rather it is better to realize that once you free yourself from a situation, you can move forward and learn from it all.

While Beatriz was controlling, she was still nice and caring in many ways. Her and I just differed in our priorities. Beatriz gifted me broaches and dresses so that I could look more elegant. It was always nice of her, but I just truly didn't care about the meaningless symbols of class that most other people spent their lives focusing on. I finally decided to leave this new home and explore the north of Spain. Beatriz tried to keep me around, but my mind was made. She was upset that I would be leaving and didn't understand why I wanted to go, but she was nice and bid me farewell.

Before traveling north, I traveled to the Moorish kingdom of Granada. I met some really welcoming people throughout my stay in Granada. During this time, Muslims were allowed to practice their religion freely, though that wouldn't last long. Eventually I headed north. I started to speak with people who told me about the lands discovered by the well-known explorer, Christopher Columbus. Sailing west, Columbus reached lands he believed to be part of Asia. I would soon realize that Asia was not where Columbus had arrived. It was 1498 when Columbus sailed on his third voyage. There was a constant buzz in the air about new lands and people. I had already explored quite a few lands that others had no real concept of. This taste of new territory was making me anxious again. The average person spent his/her life in one location, with no concept of what else was out there. They assumed their way of life was "normal," but I found that there really was no "normal" in this world. Spain was a beautiful country with so many great people, as I had found everywhere I went.

However, I had experienced that control tore people apart and only caused resentment. On a small scale, Beatriz's control over me as well as her family prevented me from ultimately respecting her as much as I wanted to. On a larger scale, Ferdinand and Isabella's attempt to control their territory only caused more turmoil. It was 1502 when the Muslims of Granada were forced to either convert or leave Spain. It wasn't any different than the anti-Semitism expressed 10 years earlier. People with power can and will control.

It was time for me to leave. All the talk about Christopher Columbus' adventures made me curious. I went west.

NINE

AN UNLIKELY FRIEND

North Atlantic Ocean

From the moment I entered the sea, I felt at home. However, I had a strange, unexplainable feeling of sadness. I was still so unsure about this world, my purpose and what it all meant. While there were some amazing people that I truly connected with, there were also so many people that I just didn't understand. I felt as if so many people had become so disconnected from nature and from what was important. Thoughts flooded my mind trying to make sense of this world. I tried to understand why so many people were so preoccupied in impressing each other with money or jewels or *things*. Rather than working as one, they were in a constant battle with each other and thus, they were in a constant battle with themselves.

I have found that everyone goes through ups and downs. Right now, I was at a down. I swam to keep my mind preoccupied. I encountered some big storms soon after leaving Spain. Every time I came up for air, the furious wind, ominous skies, and mighty waves clouded my mind further. There was a solemn feeling in the air and in the sea as the earth wailed. I felt lonely and doubtful. I still didn't know where I was going. My path was so unclear and often when there is no absolute plan ahead, it is easy to feel lost.

Far away from any land, with no idea of what would come next, I forced myself to keep going. All the different fish and sea life I encountered amazed me. All the living things around me had a purpose and a mind of their own. I came to notice the different personalities of various fish. Some were more curious, others were more timid, but all of them had a consciousness. They were living free, out in the wild, like me, with the sea at their disposal. I would look at certain fish in the eye and feel a connection with them despite our vast differences. They were living their lives right there with me.

The storms had been frequent and loud. However, they finally started to ease up. As the skies cleared, so did my mind. Despite the fact that I spent a lot of time under the ocean, I also spent a good amount of time on the surface, breathing, observing and relaxing. Now, I was feeling much more at peace as I traveled through the deep blue sea.

I vividly remember the day I encountered the creature that would become my closest friend at a time when I needed one most. Far out in the North Atlantic Ocean, with a clear sky above my head and endless water surrounding me, I saw a humpback whale right there in front of me.

The giant, majestic creature staring back at me mesmerized me as he came to the surface for air. He was so big and so beautifully patterned. It was hard to imagine the earth had such a magical creature living deep in the ocean. He looked so powerful, yet serene at the same time. When he went back under, I too submerged myself in the sea. I followed him down deeper into the water. When we stopped, we kept our distance, still staring into each other's eyes, curious about one another. He slowly moved closer to me, all the while looking right at me. I wasn't frightened at all as he came right over to me, close enough for me to reach my hand out and touch him. I felt a strong pulse rush through me as I gently put my hand on his big, strong body. This enchanting, complex being had altered my life.

I felt a strong connection to him and I'm sure he felt it too. Neither one of us felt the urge to leave the other. So we traveled together. Every day I grew closer to my new friend. I felt as if we understood each other better than many humans understand each other. I knew I was safe in his presence and I felt as if he was constantly looking after me. This huge creature guided me along on my journey.

We would spend our days exploring the ocean and our nights resting on the surface. We would float together, allowing the air to enter our bodies. As he slept at night, I often looked up at the stars, amazed and inspired by the world. In a sense, I was so at peace; I thought I could live like this forever, never setting foot on land again. However, I knew that with time, I would be ready to explore further.

It wasn't long before my new friend started to sing. He would produce beautiful noises by pushing air through his nasal cavities. Each song would last 10-20 minutes and sometimes he would spend an entire day singing. I didn't understand why he did it. The truth is, scientists still don't know exactly why male humpbacks do it. But the songs touched me in a way I can't describe.

It was winter now, and I soon realized that it was breeding season. I followed along as we started to trail a mother and her calf. At first, I didn't understand why the male was breaching, tail-slapping and singing more often than usual. I started to figure out that he was courting the female.

There came a point that I figured I should give my new friend his space. I didn't want to interfere with his mating rituals. So one day, I put my hands on him, looked him in the eyes and bid him farewell. There was a common understanding between us that I would be leaving him. It was sad- really sad. Why didn't I feel this way when I left some humans behind? I was so sad about leaving him that I almost changed my mind. He grunted trying to communicate something to me. I think he was saying goodbye. Maybe he was saying, "I'll miss you."

I went off on my own. I still wasn't quite ready to set foot on land again. I was content in the ocean.

As I explored on my own, I had a lot of time to think. An influx of emotions came over me as I spent my days and nights alone. There were times I felt excited about my future, inspired by the nature around me. And there were other times I felt an extreme sadness and almost hopelessness. I watched the sun rise every morning and set every night. I admired the twinkling stars and magical moon in the dark hours. I noticed the changing colors of the sky as storms approached and I stayed warm under the bright, gleaming sun. The earth had so many emotions it seemed.

I started to think about some of the people I had met so far on my journey. I thought about Cosimo a lot and really started to miss our conversations. I also really missed Ana, Hua, Li and Amr. I even started to remember brief conversations I had with individuals I barely knew, and for some reason they stuck with me. I wondered if certain souls were placed in my life for a reason, or if everything was completely left up to chance. The earth is chaotic and wild, but under all that is organization and peace. Where was Maka Koa now I wondered? Could her soul be elsewhere, maybe still on earth in another form, or maybe somewhere else? What happens when an individual passes away? And why was I so different from the rest?

It was evening and the sun was starting to set. I was in a trance while I watched the sky turn red as the ruby clouds roamed across the sky. I continued to contemplate the meaning of life and wondered about the individuals I met and what their significance was to me. Was every meeting just a coincidence? I got a strange feeling as I watched the dramatic clouds shift above me. All of a sudden, I saw a familiar face pop up beside me.

My humpback friend returned! How did he find me? I looked at him, touched his body and started to sob. I had never been so happy to see anyone... ever. I stretched my arms across him and hugged him for a long, long time.

This time around, it would be awhile before we departed again. We traveled together once more, for an even longer period of time than the first. We went north in the summers and back south in the winters. Season after season, I followed his pattern. I realized that he fed mostly during the summer time and saved the winter for breeding in the south. We encountered other humpbacks on our journey together. We even met a group of bottlenose dolphins that we spent some time playing with on a warm day out at sea. It was amazing watching how the humpbacks interacted with each other as well as with other species. I must have spent half a human lifetime in the ocean exploring with this whale I loved so much. I know this because he grew old right before my eyes. My young friend was no longer the same energetic being I once knew. Life grew harder for him day after day. His singing slowly ceased. I could tell that he wanted to go off on his own. I knew the time had come for me to give him his space to pass in peace. It was hard to imagine saying goodbye could be any harder than the first time around. But it was. Tears flooded my eyes as I left my best bud. This unlikely friend had come to mean the world to me. I knew he had lived a life filled with adventure, freedom, peace and happiness. In the end, I guess that's all one can really ask for. I loved him. I had always loved him and I would continue to love him.

I would later find out that after a whale dies, its body sinks to the seafloor and explodes, providing a great influx of food for a wide range of other sea creatures. It can take a whale carcass over 30 years to decompose, creating an ecosystem around the "whalefall." Bigger creatures such as sharks and hagfish eat the carcass, but what really amazes me is the fact that there are creatures that live off the decomposing body of a whale, down to the bone. Osedax, also known as "zombie worms" make their living solely off eating the bones of whales. *Everything* has a purpose. The earth has a way of working it all out. It's just a matter of tuning in to that unique purpose of yours. I still didn't know what my purpose was, but I was on the right path.

TEN

CLUTTER

———————

A New World
Florida
~1560

I washed ashore in the lush, beautiful, tropical land of Florida. This paradise was wild and charming. I immediately took a liking to the land. Clear, blue waters, sandy beaches and blossoming flowers welcomed me. I arrived in South Florida and spent some time there, getting to know the land and getting to know some of the native people that lived there.

The Native American group known as the Tequestas warmly welcomed me. They had been living on this land for close to 2000 years and they knew it well. In many ways they reminded me of the Australian aborigines I had gotten to know once upon a time. They hunted and gathered, catching a majority of their food from the sea. I loved trying different fruits that grew on the trees by the ocean. Sea grapes became my favorite.

The Tequesta people were very friendly and a very spiritual

group of people. They truly cherished the land they lived on, waking up with the sun every morning and following the patterns of the moon. Surprised by the fact I could communicate with them, they accepted me into their lives with open arms. They had only experienced brief interactions with European explorers previous to my arrival, so they were not accustomed to having outsiders join their group. I adapted well. My skin had bronzed into a mocha color and my hair was long and dark. I could almost pass for one of them. I liked that these people were simple in their ways of life. I felt at home wearing minimal clothing and feeling free to walk around barefoot. With no worries of having to cover up my body because of religion or culture, I felt free and at peace with these people and with nature.

Sisika, a young girl 16 years of age, befriended me right off the bat. She was very much free-spirited. With a zest for life and adventure constantly on her mind, she took me by the hand and led me to her favorite secret spots away from the village. Sisika sang with the birds, picked beautiful flowers to put in her hair and always admired the little creatures that scurried around us. Sisika's brother, Apenimon, was similar to Sisika in ways, but he was much more serious. Apenimon was an honest, hard-working man. He was 25 years old, but to me, he was an "old soul." The brother and sister were extremely close, and I became a friend to the both of them. All three of us would go on adventures together. Sometimes I would spend time alone with Sisika, other times I would spend time only with Apenimon, but often the three of us were inseparable.

I specifically remember the afternoon that Sisika and I went to one of her secret spots, deep in the mangrove trees. We climbed around them until we found a comfortable spot to sit and talk like we often did. I clearly recall Sisika asking me more questions than usual that day. She was curious about my past. She wondered where my parents were, if I had any siblings and where I came from. I answered as best I could, but couldn't give her any real answers since I didn't know myself. I told her I came from an island not too far away. I was honest as I told her I didn't remember much from my past and didn't even know who my parents were or if I had any siblings. She pondered my words for a little while before asking me more questions. She started asking me a lot of philosophical questions. She asked me if I thought all living things were created equal. I said "yes, I have found that every living thing has a unique purpose, whether we can clearly see that purpose or not." She seemed to agree. Sisika moved closer to me to braid my hair. She liked playing with my hair and adorning me with flowers and pretty little shells. Sometimes she even looked closely at shells on the shore, looking for one that matched the shell I wore as a ring. A bird flew overhead and she made a noise calling to it. She told me that she often dreamed of animals. Eating animals was common, but she said that sometimes she felt bad taking the life of an animal for food. I listened to her and appreciated her words. This was something I thought about often. I lived a simple life and was able to care for myself by eating very little amounts of seaweed, fruits and grains. I didn't need meat to survive, however, I ate what was placed in front of me whenever I lived with various people around the world. I knew that on this planet, everything eats everything. That is the way of life. And that is okay, when everything is in balance. Everything lives and everything dies. I told all of this to Sisika as she continued to braid my hair. "Moderation is key," I said. "Take what you need, don't be wasteful and always appreciate the food in front of you."

Life was abundant back then. The sad truth was that everything would start to change very quickly soon after. There would no longer be "moderation." Life would no longer be valued the same way it was.

As I stayed with the Tequesta tribe, I started to have many dreams again. Dreams were very important to these people, much like the aborigines I lived with in Australia. My dreams were a jumble of information. My mind started to feel cluttered as I tried to process all the thoughts in my head. I often woke up anxious and confused. It felt as if so much was happening at once and I couldn't tap into what it meant. So many people I had met along the way spoke to me in my sleep. I didn't know if any of it was of significance to me or if it was all just a bunch of information jumbled together with no real meaning.

I spoke to Apenimon about my dreams. I had found that Apenimon always offered sound advice. He was levelheaded and had his wits about him. I told him I felt unsure and confused, in life as well as in my dreams. It seemed to me that something big was about to happen, but right now everything seemed stagnant. I couldn't figure out what would happen next.

The year was 1565 when a man named Menéndez arrived. There was a bad storm so Menéndez and his crew took refuge in Biscayne Bay. The Tequestas welcomed him and his crew, as they did with me. It was a strange thing to watch these European men interact with these primitive people. It almost seemed like two different species coming together. Overall, the interactions were friendly ones. Menéndez had a bunch of Jesuits with him. These religious men seemed to want to educate the native people on Christianity. They seemed to have the Tequesta's best interest in mind. When the Jesuits departed, they took the chief's nephew back to Havana, Cuba to be educated. The chief's brother accompanied Menéndez back to Spain where he would convert to Christianity. Menéndez would found Saint Augustine that year, the oldest city in the continental United States.

When the European men departed, things went back to normal with the Tequestas. I continued to live amongst them and continued to spend my days with Sisika and Apenimon. I felt a strong connection to each of them. Sometimes I got the feeling that Apenimon liked me as more than just a friend, but I wasn't quite sure.

It was years before we would encounter Spanish men again, but I distinctly remember when it happened. It was March of 1567 when Menéndez returned. Near the south bank of the Miami River, below our village, Menéndez established a mission. Brother Francisco and 30 soldiers were here to stay to try to convert the Tequestas to Christianity.

Things started changing. Not necessarily in a bad way, but not necessarily in a good way. My dreams came back, cluttering my mind more and more as so many things started to happen.

It was dusk and the sky was pinkish blue. It was slightly foggy and there was a faint wind that chilled my skin. As I slowly made my way amongst the mangroves, I suddenly encountered a Spanish soldier. His name was Philip. I stared, attracted to him in a strange way. He had a look in his eye as he stared back at me, seeming to be drawn to me. He spoke to me in Spanish, with the slight chance that I would understand. I definitely did not look Spanish considering I wore next to nothing. However, I guess I didn't quite look like one of the Tequestas either. Of course I understood and of course he was surprised.

Upon meeting Philip, I could tell that he was a good guy. He didn't look threatening at all. I have found that upon initially meeting someone, you can often get a pretty good feeling about what kind of person they are, just based off instinct. For me at least, this has always been a technique that seems to work.

Philip and I had just met, but somehow we ended up sitting amongst the mangroves and having a conversation. That conversation turned into a long one as the pink sky faded into black. He was here with Brother Francisco on a mission. Philip was religious. He was a Christian man. He was a good man. He was surprised when I told him I had lived in Spain and I think that drew him to me even more. It wasn't easy trying to explain how I made my way this far across the ocean to come live with the Native Americans but I tried to keep my stories brief by asking him more questions than he asked me.

Over time, I got to know Philip more and more. The Spanish men would come in to the village to create relations with the Native Americans. I became a sort of "middle man" between the two very different groups. The Spanish had a lot to teach the Tequestas. Much of what the Spanish preached was good and the native people learned a fair amount about "civilized life." Some Tequestas were more open to the idea of Christianity, while others were happy with their current ways. Many Tequestas even thought of the Europeans as "gods" and were very much influenced by them, willing to be converted.

Apenimon was one who was happy with his current way of life. In ways we grew closer once the Spanish arrived. Apenimon expressed his concern over the loss of his peoples' ways of life to these European men who thought they were "right" in their ways. I agreed that the Europeans were often forceful and less open minded than they could be. However, I also felt as if maybe there was a way both groups could work together and have an open, friendly style of communication so that everyone benefited from what the others had to offer.

I started spending more and more time with Philip as well. I started to feel as if I was dividing my days between Philip and Apenimon. Both of these men offered a different point of view and I respected each of these men equally. However, with time, I felt that each of them wanted more than just a friendship with me.

One night, Apenimon presented me with a gift. He hand-carved a bracelet for me out of a seashell! He knew how much

I cherished the shell ring I wore on my pinky and I guess that's what inspired his creation. I was overjoyed with the gift. It really put a smile on my face. I hugged Apenimon and gave him a kiss on the cheek, appreciating the effort he put into my gift.

When I showed Philip the bracelet Apenimon had made for me, I could sense a jealousy. The very next day, Philip presented me with a bouquet of flowers he picked on his way to the village. They were lovely, but I knew something was up. My mind continued to fill with clutter as these two, very different men, tried to win me over. There was a tension between the two of them and I felt it as well. As Philip tugged me in one direction and Apenimon in the other, I felt as if I was being torn apart. My mind was frazzled.

Brother Francisco won over some converts from the Tequestas, but it was a slow process. I still don't know exactly what happened, but the day that everything changed was when some soldiers executed an uncle of the chief. That was it for Apenimon. He didn't want me to go anywhere near Philip. I told Apenimon that Philip was not involved in any way, but Apenimon wouldn't hear it.

Philip truly thought he was doing a good deed by showing the native people how to live a more efficient, civilized, moral life. There were things I liked about the European way of life. I understood Philip and I grew to really care about him. He was truly a *good* person. Yet, I understood Apenimon's point of view as well. He didn't understand why these Europeans were over here trying to improve on something that didn't need fixing. Things were just fine without their help.

My dreams grew more confusing as I was being pulled in so many different directions. Brother Francisco was forced to abandon the mission for a while because of the execution. However, when the chief's brother returned from Spain, brother Francisco was able to come back.

Things started to fall apart not only in my own mind, but amongst these two groups of people as well. The mission was abandoned in 1570, just a few years after it began. I said goodbye to Philip, a man who became my good friend. I was sad to see him leave, but it was for the best. Apenimon couldn't be happier.

I never had anything more than a friendship with either Philip or Apenimon. I think that is best. While I knew each of them liked me, it wasn't worth starting something with either of these men that I didn't see any sort of future with. It would have created more tension and problems. My mind was cluttered up enough as it was.

I stayed with the Tequestas a little while longer. I had grown to love them and their way of life. I had a family once again. Leaving, as always, was difficult. But there was more out there. I was sure of it.

ELEVEN

PART OF THE PACK

North America
1572

Once I left the Tequestas, I bounced around for a while. I traveled by ocean along the coast of Florida, often venturing inland, exploring all the unbelievable nature Florida had to offer. Not too far north of where I had been living, I found the most magical, blue, springs. I spent a lot of time swimming in the crystal waters, dancing underwater with the other type of "mermaids," known as manatees. Prehistoric looking trees shaded the teal waters abundant with the majestic manatees. Ever amazed with this earth, I kept moving along, always encountering mystical places I couldn't believe to be real. The further north I traveled, the cooler the air became. I was leaving the tropics. There were various natives living throughout the areas I traveled. I mingled with some of them but never stayed too long in one place.

I followed rivers up through dense forests and rocky land leading me to stunning waterfalls and more magical places. I collected clothing and gifts from various Native Americans I met along the way. Many of these tribes thought I was a goddess as I left them just as quickly as I came.

I spent a lot of time alone, out in the wilderness, following the rising sun and the patterns of the moon. I felt a deep, spiritual connection to the earth. I listened to all the sounds of nature. Sometimes while I slept at night, I heard wolves howling up at the black sky. I had seen these beautiful creatures from a distance and I admired them from afar. However, it wouldn't be long before I would no longer be a stranger to these exquisite animals.

One night, while I dreamed of lands I had yet to see, I awoke to a wet, slobber across my face. Uneasy, I jumped up to find a big gray wolf looking right at me. I had watched these creatures hunt bigger prey than themselves, so it was only natural for me to feel apprehensive in their presence. However, I realized pretty quickly that the wolf right in front of me had no intent to make me his midnight snack. It was quite the opposite actually. This wolf was curious about me. Usually wolves are scared of humans, more scared of humans than humans are of them. Yet, for whatever reason, this wolf got up the courage to come over and awaken me from my sleep with his kiss on my face. I looked at him and looked away, repeatedly for a few moments, unsure of what he wanted. Eventually, he inched closer and then started rubbing his entire body over mine. Nervous at first, after a couple of minutes I went with it, embracing him in my arms.

This alpha male liked me enough to take me in. Strangely enough, this next phase of my life would involve a new type of family for me. Welcomed into the pack, I was the newest addition to this wolf family. As the leader of the pack, the alpha male always got what he wanted. And he wanted me around.

There were eight of us total: seven canine friends and I. We traveled together far and wide. I was protected and loved by these big, cuddly creatures. It was so interesting to watch these animals. I learned a lot about them and their ways of life. There was an alpha male in charge of the pack. There was also an alpha female. These were the only two that bred. Then there were other wolves that varied in dominance levels. I vividly remember the day that the alpha female gave birth to the most adorable pups I had ever seen. Her four newborns were so small, born without sight or hearing (as all wolf pups are born). The mom looked after them at first, but after a month or so, I would spend time watching the pups in the den while their mom went out and hunted. Moving from den to den every few months, I watched the dedicated mom care for the only thing in the world that mattered to her. These pups were her life. They became the most important thing in all of our lives. I watched these babies grow bigger and bigger by the day. It was the most amazing thing.

I really grew to love these creatures. I became exceptionally close with one of the wolf pups. I loved them all but I formed a special connection with one I named Adelpha. She had a unique black spot on her nose that almost looked like a heart. Adelpha loved me as much as I loved her. We would have done anything for one another. I loved listening to the pack howl to one another. It was amazing to hear them communicate, pulling the pack together and letting each other know what was happening in the area. The way they communicated using body language was fascinating as well. The lower ranking wolves would crouch in the presence of a higher-ranking wolf. There was a definite hierarchy and each wolf had its own place in their society. It worked for them. It was incredible.

It is a weird feeling writing about these memories. It brings back all these feelings I once had. Centuries later, I would try to explain to people about my relationship to these amazing animals, but many people didn't understand or maybe didn't believe me. Today, people realize the importance of wolves, but for a while, wolves were treated as man's worst enemy.

Wolves were brought almost to extinction by "civilization" only a couple hundred years later. It was painful to see people on a rampage to kill these amazing animals. Wolves were hunted not only for their fur, but also because wolves preyed on the herds of domestic animals. I remember wolf hunters used Strychnine, a poison placed in the dead carcasses of buffalo, sheep, or cattle. Wolves (as well as coyotes, dogs, and many other animals) would die a painful death from the poisoned flesh. It sickened me to see these loyal, regal, important creatures suffering for no reason. People can be so cruel.

A few years went by before some of the wolf pups were old enough to break away from the pack and form another pack in a nearby territory. I had formed such a strong bond with these wolves and I became even more compassionate toward animals and their significance to this earth. I think that many people believe they are more important than other living things. However, I have found that we all play an important role on this planet, no matter if you are a human, a wolf, a sea turtle, or even an ant. *Every living thing* is just as important as the next. This is something people have yet to figure out.

When the pups broke away from the pack, so did I. I had learned so much from their complex community and I was changed once again. This journey taught me something new every single day and I was moving in the right direction whether I realized it or not.

Saying goodbye to this family was just as difficult as saying goodbye to any human family I had lived with. They knew I was leaving. I was especially sad to leave Adelpha. She rubbed her big furry body all over mine before bidding me farewell. She whimpered a bit and howled. The connection we had was one that couldn't be broken. I would remember her and the rest of the pack for as long as I lived. I loved them. They were my family.

TWELVE

THE TIME I GOT CAUGHT

Pacific Ocean
1579

I traveled west across North America for many years after departing from the wolf pack. The land was truly remarkable. I ventured from mountains to grasslands and prairies and then back to mountains before reaching the sea. I felt the air change and the seasons come and go. Once again, I fell madly in love with the rich land I spent so much time venturing on. All different communities of plants and animals encompassed the vast areas of land I crossed.

Again I encountered various native people along the way, but never stayed in one place for too long. I was happy to be on my own exploring at my own pace. I took my time, enjoying. I was in no rush to get anywhere. I didn't have anywhere to go. Where does anyone ever really have to go anyways? After a long time of wandering, I made it to present day California. I reached the coast and the Pacific Ocean was a glorious site. I was back to the sea at last.

I dove into the ocean, feeling my fin form once again. What a truly unbelievable world this was. I had experienced so much already, yet it felt as if my journey had just begun. I splashed salt water on my face and filled my mouth with the ocean to taste the sea again. I felt light and liberated.

I swam for a while with no intent to return to land just yet. I spent many days just floating, looking up at the sky. I dove deep down into the sea living moment by moment. I was in a playful mood. I was excited but I didn't know exactly what I was excited about. I guess I was just excited to live, to be alive, and experience everything I could.

I was feeling positive and ready for whatever life had in store for me. However, nothing could have prepared me for what would happen next. It was early in the morning and light had just started to creep into the sky. I was fast asleep, floating on the surface of the water. I was deep in a dream, a dream I no longer remember. I awoke to find myself in the most frightened state I have yet to experience.

I don't know how I didn't wake up sooner, but it all happened so fast. I woke up just as a giant net was hauling me out of the water. A bunch of men were in the boat, yelling excitedly. I was terrified.

I was released from the net on the deck of the boat. I looked up at the group of gnarly looking pirates staring straight at me. I was shaking in the silence. I don't think anyone knew what to say or think. My fin was now a pair of legs and the pirates didn't know what to make of their latest find.

In a state of panic, I jumped up with the intent to dash for the water. I wasn't quick enough. One of the men grabbed me, holding me back from escaping. I looked at the surrounding men, looking deep into their eyes, looking for some sort of sympathy. I didn't know what these pirates had in mind, but I wasn't too keen to find out.

The man holding me back pulled me in tighter. His grip was so strong and he smelled of booze and unwashed skin. One man yelled out "looks like we got ourselves a new crewmate, ehh!" The others started to laugh. Just then, another spoke out. "Give her to me," he said. The others looked at him and the man holding me obeyed with a "yes, sir." I could tell that this man was in charge. He took me by the arm and told me to follow him. I did (not that I really had any other choice.) We went into the captain's quarters of the large wooden ship.

This man told me his name was Francis. He asked if I understood. I said "yes." I told him my name was Annala. He smiled, looking at me inquisitively. He asked me, "Who, or rather *what* are you my lady?" Nervously, I replied, "I don't know."

"I don't know anything about you young lady, but I like you. I do not wish to cause you any harm. There are a good number of hungry men aboard this ship who have not seen women for a long time now. I don't know if you understand what I am trying to tell you, but something gives me the feeling that I should let you free."

He looked at me, trying to read the expression on my face. He waited for my reply, but I sat there in silence, looking up at him. I could tell that he was a strong, maybe even brutal man. But he also had a kindness.

I was no longer so afraid. I asked him where he came from. He laughed and said, "That is not easy to answer." After a quick pause he continued, "I was most recently off the coast of Peru. You caught me in a good mood. I just captured the treasure ship, *Nuestra Señora de la Concepción*. Naturally, I am very pleased, as this is an extremely profitable capture!" He smiled and then said, "But you are probably looking for a more simple answer. I am from Britain." He looked down at my hand and I watched him notice my shell ring. "What is that you wear on your finger?" I took it off and handed it to him as I said, "it is a shell I found." He fumbled it around in his hands, halfway seeing if it would fit him, yet knowing all the while it wouldn't. He handed it back and said, "You have small fingers." I shrugged while putting it back on my pinky, looking at it.

Francis stared at me, wonderingly. "I have been at sea a long time. We all have. Sometimes I think this way of life drives a man mad. Yet, I am fairly certain of what I saw out in the water this morning."

I didn't know what to say to him. I just kept staring at him, almost blankly. He kept looking at me before speaking again. "You know, I have heard about creatures like you. But I was always doubtful. Other explorers and seamen have reported sightings, yet I had never experienced it for myself. You are lovely. I get the feeling you have powers beyond your knowledge." He pulled out a bracelet from a chest filled with gold and jewels. He held it up with his thumb and index finger looking at it before looking back at me. "I want you to have this my dear. I acquired this Inca gold bracelet from my most recent Spanish capture. This particular bracelet looks special to me, which is why I want you to have it."

He handed it to me. "Thank you," I said. He smiled and shook his head. "We live in a world full of wonders. There is much darkness, but you are a light. Keep that light about you." I looked at him and I couldn't help but smile. Not but an hour ago I was scared to death. Now, here I was with this captain gifting me Inca jewels. I felt lucky. I felt as if something much bigger than myself was watching me, guiding me and showing me a way.

A seaman came to the captain's quarters. "Captain Drake," he said, "we have spotted a good port. Shall we land to repair and restock the vessel?" Francis replied, "Yes good man, we shall. I will be right out." The seaman glanced over at me, looking deep into my soul. I looked back. All these connections we make, even just for a few seconds, seem to mean something. Once the seaman left, Francis looked at me and told me, "It would be best if you left." I agreed.

Francis accompanied me out to a desolate area of the large ship. All the men were congregated at the bow. I snuck off from the side. Right before I jumped overboard, I looked at Francis, and then almost instinctively, embraced him in a hug. I was grateful for my release and I felt some weird special force between us. He gave me a slow pat on the back and then hugged me a little tighter. I looked into his eyes one last time before departing the ship.

I don't know what Francis said to his men about me. For some reason, I don't think he revealed too much.

I was free again and it felt amazing. So much had happened this morning and it was hard to wrap my head around all of it. My heart was beating fast as I swam away from the ship. I thought about what Francis had said about "creatures like me." Were there others? I wanted to find out. It was my new mission. I looked down at my gifted bracelet, smiled and then started my adventure southbound through the comforting sea.

THIRTEEN

SKETCHES, STRANGE CREATURES & AN ANYTHING BUT ORDINARY PIRATE

———

The Galapagos
~1650-1685

I had so many thoughts running through my head as I started journeying south through the ocean. I couldn't stop thinking about my most recent experience with Francis and his crew. Was I just lucky in my escape? Or was freedom my destiny? I didn't know what to make of any of it. Most of all I couldn't stop thinking about the "mermaid sightings" other seamen had reported!

I tried to stay aware as I continued on my journey. The last thing I wanted was to be caught again with the slim chance of getting away the second time around. As I traveled through the sea, I kept my eyes open for others like me. My eyes started playing tricks on me. I'd see a fin and immediately get excited only to realize it was a pod of dolphins. Or I'd see something bobbing on the surface of the water and assume another mermaid was floating through the waves. However, I always ended up disappointed as days, months, and years went by without ever encountering another like me.

Yet, I tried to stay positive as I continued on my way. I had good days, bad days and many in between. I experienced a range of emotions as I watched fish swim in schools around me, listened to dolphins communicate underwater, and observed octopi change colors right before my eyes. Each creature was living its own life, doing its thing, moving along.

On a foggy morning, I spotted the islands that would cast a spell on me. The misty air masked the islands ahead. I watched the land disappear and appear through the cloudy fog. The islands looked mystical and eerie. As I moved in closer, I became entranced. This new place was thrilling. Sea lions gracefully brushed against me, giant sea turtles swam right beside me and sharks darted by in swift movements. At first, I was slightly uneasy approaching the set of islands. Yet, after a while, the Galapagos became my sanctuary. I explored all the different islands and was left in awe at the variety of wildlife that called these islands their home. Elegant flamingos brightened the land, penguins waddled by, various types of iguanas basked in the sun, giant tortoises slowly meandered around, sea lions and fur seals playfully danced and so many kinds of beautiful birds ventured through the air and land.

I spent as much time on the islands as I did in the surrounding sea. There was such a variety of plants and animals in such a small area. It was unbelievable. Every single place I went left me in awe. I may not have found other mermaids, but I certainly found some cool looking creatures.

I also continued to discover more and more about my own body. I was now able to control my fin while in the water. If I wished to swim with feet, I was able. I could transform my fin into feet and feet into fin at my own discretion. It was liberating.

I got a strange feeling as I spent more and more time on the enchanting islands. It wasn't long before I would no longer be the only person washed ashore on these beautiful islands. I very vividly remember my second encounter with pirates. This time around, the men wouldn't be so kind and understanding. It was a foggy morning but it wasn't hard to see the large ship approaching in the distance. Pirates preying on Portuguese and Spanish galleons laden with gold were here to take refuge. When they finally reached land, I made sure I was far enough away so that nobody would notice me. I kept my distance for a while. I tried to keep an eye on these men from afar but fog often prevented me from getting a clear view. Eventually, curiosity overtook me. I started to move in closer, wondering what these men were doing and where they came from.

One morning, I mustered enough courage to wash up on the island the pirates now inhabited. All the men were sleeping and the sun had yet to rise. I crept around observing these pirates that looked sunburnt, salty and unshaven. One particular pirate had fallen asleep quite close to the ocean shore. Waves moved in and out, soaking the boots on his feet every so often. He almost looked dead in his deep sleep. I was not even a foot away from him, staring right at him. It didn't look like he was waking up anytime soon. He said something in his sleep that I couldn't quite make out. I watched his arm twitch right before he scratched at his beard. I must have been in a trance, because I was so engrossed in watching this man sleep, I failed to notice the pirate approaching me from my right corner. He moved right up next to me. I don't know whose face expressed more shock upon locking eyes, his or mine. His jaw dropped as he came right over to me close enough to touch me. I didn't run. Finally, he spoke. "What in god's name are you doing out here, pretty girl?" My answer came without a second thought. "I live here," I said.

He raised an eyebrow. Just then, the sleeping pirate on the sand below awoke in a state of panic and confusion.

The no-longer sleeping pirate started cursing and mumbling before jumping up and startling me. He was still drunk from the night before. He took a swig from his flask, which wasn't about to help sober him up in any way. He surprisingly didn't seem shocked to have a female standing before him. In fact, he was quite comfortable with me there. He proceeded to grab me and tried to kiss me. I tried pushing him off and when I realized I couldn't, I started to scream. The other pirate standing right beside me didn't do anything to stop his drunken comrade. I tried to get away but was unable. As the pirate became more aggressive, I became more and more fearful about what might happen. He wasn't letting me go and his friend seemed to be encouraging it! Couldn't they tell I wasn't happy? Why didn't they care? I had encountered some selfish and vile people on my journey so far, but I had never been in a situation like this. Usually, I was very trusting of people and usually people gave me every reason to trust them. I had found that most would help me out if they could. Most people did not have the intention to hurt me. But these men only had *their* best interests in mind, with no thought of what *I* wanted.

The intoxicated pirate started to fumble with his pants buckle. I immediately reacted by striking him hard where his hands had wandered down. I had never hit someone before but I had no choice. He yelped as I ran past the two pirates and sought my haven, the ocean. I was so shaken up and didn't want to go anywhere near any pirate for a long time. I was lucky that I was able to get away, but I was still frightened. I didn't go back on the land that these pirates inhabited until they finally left. I continued to live on the surrounding islands, constantly keeping my eyes open and aware. It was such a relief when I finally saw the pirates' ship departing.

I was content to be alone with just the surrounding wildlife to keep me company. I grew close to the playful sea lions that loved hanging out around me. They were curious, social and whimsical animals. I adored them. I felt at peace on these magical islands once again.

I lived on the islands for years and years. Every now and then a ship would appear with a group of pirates taking refuge on the islands. I always kept my distance. I was afraid. I had lost my trust and I didn't want to put myself in a situation I was uncomfortable with. I hated seeing a ship enter the island area. The longer I stayed on the islands, the more they felt like home and whenever I saw a ship full of pirates, I always assumed they'd be the same drunken, dirty type men I had problems with the last time around. I also noticed that many of these people had no regard for the land they had arrived on and the animals living here. Desperate for food, I often watched these men slaughter tons of sea lions and tortoises that I had gotten to know so well. It is one thing to eat for survival. Everything lives and everything dies. However, I noticed that many of these men were wasteful and didn't seem to regard these animals' lives as important. It angered me to see some of the oldest, biggest animals get slaughtered and then thrown out. As I had once told my young friend, Sisika, "moderation is key." I think it is important to take what you need and have appreciation for it, without wasting and losing regard for other living things.

The longer I kept my distance from any humans, the more fearful I became. What if the men captured and raped me? What if they killed me? What if they took me as a prisoner? What if's occupied my mind to the point that I wanted to spend the rest of my existence free from human contact.

It's funny how the longer you distance yourself from something, the more scary and foreign it seems. It reminded me of my early life spent in the South Pacific. While in a sense, I was curious about the earth, I was too comfortable in my sphere of the ocean. I could have easily stayed in the South Pacific and been content for my entire life. However, looking back, I realized that I had seen and experienced so much, and all of those experiences were so worth me leaving my initial "home." As I continued to think about my life and the experiences I had with other humans, I realized that my fear was not something that should hold me back. Of course I should be careful, but maybe it was time for me to start trusting again.

The year was 1679 and a new ship had entered the Galapagos. Now was the time for me to face my fear. Pirates might be brutal and rugged but Francis had proven that they could be kind and forgiving as well. The anything but ordinary pirate waiting for me on the next island over would reinforce this thought.

I watched the buccaneers from a safe spot in the water for a while before deciding to finally step foot on land with them. This group of pirates seemed to be close to one another. I determined that they were in a somewhat peaceful period, as I didn't observe much fighting or yelling going on amongst them. There was one particular pirate that would go off on his own, observing the land and recording stuff in his journal. While many of the pirates I had observed in the past stayed on only one island, this group seemed curious enough to explore deeper into the Galapagos with their smaller boats.

It was a sunny day, and I was feeling adventurous. I swam along the shore of the island keeping an eye on the pirate that was so deeply focused on his journal. I splashed around a little, but he didn't notice me. As I watched him, I took a liking to him. He didn't look like many of the other typical drunk fighters I had observed in the past. He looked inquisitive and interested in the land.

We were far away from the other men on his ship. I felt safe in the presence of this one man. A group was more intimidating, but this one didn't scare me. He was sitting on the shore, observing a bird intently as he scribbled away at the paper in front of him. I slowly moved closer to him. My body was halfway out of the shallow water, when I caught his eye. The sun was right behind me and I caught him squinting in disbelief as I approached. His hand stopped moving as he stared at me, probably wondering if he was awake or dreaming. I don't know what got in to me, but I was not afraid, not even in the slightest. I walked right over to him and sat down on the sand next to him. I looked at him, smiled and introduced myself as Annala. It took him a minute to reply but finally he muttered "Dampier, William Dampier." He just kept staring and it was then that I laughed in disbelief at my own nervousness previous to this new meeting.

Finally, he said "I'm sorry, but who are you?" "I live here," I said. "These islands are my home." I looked over at his journal, trying to get a look before asking, "What are you putting down in there?" He flipped through a few pages as he said "just some notes and sketches." I got a quick glance before he shut the notebook.

Dampier became more comfortable with me as he accepted the fact that he was not dreaming. "I'm extremely confused. Where did you come from?" I laughed again and then said, "Meet me back here tomorrow. But promise you won't tell another soul about me?" He stared and then nodded in confusion and agreement. I walked away until I was out of his sight and then jumped back in the water. Until tomorrow...

That night I observed Dampier while hiding in the sea. I could tell he had a lot on his mind. He didn't spend much time conversing with the other pirates. Rather, he was preoccupied in his own thoughts, probably thinking about our mysterious meeting.

The next morning, before the sun lit up the sky, I watched Dampier leave his camp before the other men awoke. As he walked along the shore, I followed along by way of the ocean, making sure he didn't see me. When he made it to "our spot," he sat down and waited. I swam around to an area a little further down before exiting the water. I walked along the shore until I reached him. He stood up when he saw me approaching.

Our conversation started out slow and awkward, but eventually, we couldn't stop talking. This man seemed to have wisdom beyond his years. He told me he was 28 years old, but I felt as if he was as old as I was! What I liked most about him was his curiosity. He was born in England but had already sailed on two merchant voyages and would go on to circumnavigate the earth 3 times! He was extremely observant and constantly wrote down his thoughts and discoveries. This initial conversation turned into us meeting every day.

William became my good friend. I really liked him. He was motivated, inquisitive and intelligent beyond his years. I even developed a slight crush on him (though I never acted upon it). He told me that he didn't want to tell any of his fellow crewmates about me. I thought that was a good idea. So we continued to meet in secret.

As days went by, we went together to different islands. He would paddle us around in his small boat and I would show him all the different species I had spent time observing. He was amazed by it all, constantly writing and drawing. His sketches were unbelievable. I was already a writer, putting thoughts and notes into my journal regularly, but I had never really sketched before. He inspired me to start drawing. His sketches were always much more detailed and elaborate than mine, but sketching would become something I would continue to do throughout my travels.

Dampier was a difficult man for me to read. I really started to develop feelings for him, but he never made any advances toward me. He became my best friend and we really opened up to each other. It's funny how you can go months, years, or decades without forming a strong connection with someone. But then, all of a sudden, in a matter of days, you can form a bond that will last forever. I never told Dampier that I was a mermaid, but I think he knew. He definitely knew I was not a normal human being.

Soon enough, Dampier and his crew needed to be on their way. I was really devastated he would be leaving. I felt as if I was just getting to know him. However, he promised me he would be back.

He left and I waited. I often thought about him. Sometimes I worried he would never return. I had never been so attached to someone I barely knew before. He had cast a spell on me. The islands had also cast a spell on me. I had no intention of leaving these wonderful bodies of land anytime soon. Years went by and

Dampier had yet to return. Every time a new ship came near, I always got excited, hoping my friend was back. It was five years before he would return.

In 1684, Dampier anchored at Buccaneer Cove on Santiago Island. This time around he was with a different group of men. When I laid eyes on him again, I was overwhelmed with excitement. As soon as he and the rest of the crew set foot on land, I observed Dampier constantly looking around, looking for me. The first night the men built a fire, cooked up some tortoise meat and then called it a night. The very next day, before sunrise, Dampier was waiting for me at the same spot we had met 5 years earlier. The smile on my face left no room for questioning how elated I was to see him again.

Things were exactly as they were years before. He was the same man, just with infinitely more experiences under his belt. He was excited and talkative. He told me about Captain John Cook and navigator William Cowley, the men he was currently on board with. He laughed as he told me that they renamed their recently seized Danish ship, the Bachelor's Delight. He told me that he insisted on stopping here in the Galapagos. The men on board didn't understand why he wanted to stop here so desperately. He looked at me and winked. My heart sunk. I smiled at him. He had so many stories about his adventures as he had circumnavigated the globe since our last meeting!

Dampier was so enamored by the variety of species. He noted all the little differences between the green sea turtles he encountered here versus in the Caribbean. The spiked lizards and giant tortoises could keep him interested for hours on end. I loved his drive and passion. There are not that many people that have such a passion for life.

One night, we were sitting on a rock by the edge of the ocean. Our conversations had grown deeper as we spent weeks together again. I felt so at home in his presence. On this particular night he mentioned something to me he had never mentioned before. He mentioned a wife he had at home. I don't know why I was jealous since there had never been any romantic happenings between us, but I was. He didn't say anything about her, he just mentioned her in passing. I never probed.

Dampier loved pushing my limits. He would tease me and joke around, more than any other man had attempted before him. I liked it. He thought it was so interesting watching the pouches of the male frigate birds inflate to attract females. He took note of the mating habits of various animals. Dampier was charming. He was eloquent in his speech and his writings. I learned a great deal from him. I was so attracted to *his mind*.

Time went by and his men were soon ready to continue on their journey. They had explored the islands and even drew a map of the land. I never interacted with any of them, but Dampier always told me stories about the men on his ship. They seemed like decent guys overall, though to me, nobody would ever come close to being as exquisite as Dampier.

When it came time for Dampier to leave, I became anxious and sad. I felt as if he was leaving me behind. However, I knew that he must be on his way. He told me he would return again.

Dampier left and my world was shattered. Why was I so distraught over this man leaving? We had never had anything more than a friendship. I thought about waiting around for him to return. However, I knew in my heart that I should leave as well. The world was waiting and there was so much more for me to see.

I never saw Dampier again, however, I heard he returned to the Galapagos one last time. I'd like to think he was looking for me.

FOURTEEN

CONNECTED TO SOMETHING BIG

The Amazon
~1700

When I left the Galapagos, I had a sad feeling. This beautiful land was now what I knew and it was difficult leaving many of the animals I had befriended behind. However, it was time. I traveled through the ocean for a little while but before too long I found the land I was meant to travel next.

I first traveled through the coastal desert of Peru, feeling the dry air and hot sun bake my skin. I continued inland, crossing the Andean highlands where I observed so many types of beautiful bright birds, the cutest foxes and wooly vicuñas. There were tons of various species of birds, reptiles and mammals living in the Andes and it was amazing to see so many animals I had yet to see anywhere else in the world.

It was extremely strenuous climbing the Andes. Every single day was a challenge. The high altitudes made it difficult to catch my breath. I found that chewing on coca leaves helped, but didn't ease the pain in my legs and back as I used muscles not needed in the ocean. However, I grew strong and when I reached the top, the feeling was unexplainable. I rested on top of the Andes for a while, viewing the vast Pacific Ocean and desert land on one side, and the bright greens of the widespread Amazon on the other side. I was heading toward the wet, lush forest and I was looking forward to the change. I admired the very different lands as I looked out from above. There was such a wide range of landscapes on both sides. It was amazing.

Eventually, I reached the Amazon. This vast, extensive rainforest was intimidatingly wonderful. So many sounds filled the air day and night. I was not alone in this divine land. Trees towered above me as I followed along the flowing river. The strangest looking insects occupied the land and air, tree frogs hopped from leaf to leaf, giant fish swam through the rippling water, curious monkeys howled from the treetops, the brightest, most colorful birds soared above me, and elegant jaguars slowly made their way through the enchanting forest, always keeping an eye on me. I should have been more nervous than I was. I would later find out that this rainforest held quite a few species that could harm or kill me with just a touch. However, right now I was confident as I trekked through the trees day after day.

All the various plants mesmerized me as I looked closely at the intricate patterns and colors. There were a variety of greens surrounding me with a multitude of colors splattered in between. At night I heard all kinds of critters communicating through the darkness. I always awoke as the sun first started to shine through the trees above me, glistening through the leafy roof.

Big furry spiders, huge bullet ants and so many other types of insects crept around me. Earth is filled with magic. Soon enough, my magical world would become even more magical than I could have imagined.

I traveled deep into the Amazon until I reached a village of natives. I walked over to the village, not really knowing what to expect from the people living in this remote rainforest. The people were timid toward me at first. They were not unfriendly, they were just wary. I spoke to them and as they realized I was not there to cause them any harm, they warmed up to me.

I started to live with these people. They caught fish from the river, hunted, and ate the plentiful fruits and vegetables of the land. They took me in without asking me any questions. I think they believed I was a celestial being, as did many of the other natives I had encountered in my travels. I befriended a young girl who everyone called Ti. Ti was youthful but extremely wise. She had endured a few health problems growing up, having more near death experiences than most her age. While physically she looked fragile, her mind was strong. Amongst these people, she was a young, practicing shaman. Her dreams often showed her things of importance to other tribe members. She spoke to me about life, our "reality," dreams, death, and other states of existence. I was fascinated by how this young girl had so much knowledge of various plants and how they affect the human brain. She told me about a particular fungus that had powerful effects on us. I became more and more fascinated and curious as she continued to tell me about her experiences with the fungus. Ti and I had a strong connection. I could tell that Ti saw wisdom in me, similar to how I saw it in her, just in a different way. As I expressed more interest in the mushrooms, she encouraged me to try them when I felt ready.

I very vividly remember the first time I tried them. It was a beautiful day. Ti warned me that the flavor was not very pleasant and that I may feel uncomfortable, even nauseous at first.

She had tried to describe what it *felt* like to be on shrooms, but words can only resonate so much. You can *try* to understand it with words. However, in order to truly understand something, one must actually *feel* it.

I ate them, and lay outside by the river, by myself, waiting to feel something. It took about an hour or so to hit me. I remember looking up at the sky and all of a sudden I felt as if something was trying to tell me something. I then looked down at my own legs and saw them breathing and moving, almost like snakeskin. I stayed out there a little while longer until a couple of village girls wandered by me and said hi. They looked distorted to me. It was weird. Soon after, Ti came by to check on me. I followed her inside one of the huts. I remember looking down at the beautiful Inca gold bracelet Francis had gifted me and I started to laugh. Ti asked me what I was laughing at. I told her "it's funny, for some reason, previous to me eating the mushrooms, I assumed while on mushrooms, I would look down at the bracelet and it would mean something. Maybe it would look much more beautiful or feel magical in some way. But no, it's just a bracelet!" I continued to laugh as she smiled and said, "I know."

I sat down on a bed in the hut, thoughts flooding my mind. All of a sudden I started to laugh and cry as I realized how beautiful and amazing life is. I felt lucky. I lay down and started to talk. I closed my eyes and felt as if I was shooting through space. I spilled my heart out to Ti as she listened to all the realizations I was having.

I remember telling her that it wasn't me "Annala" that was speaking. Something else was speaking through me. I told her that "they" wanted her to know something. I couldn't quite get one particular message across. The only thing I could tell her was that she was on the right path. Occasionally I would look at her and see her as a true shaman. This was what she was *meant* to do. I felt as if the earth was moving toward something. We were moving toward something big. I kept saying, "there is a truth" as I pointed up at the sky. I was reassured that "trust" was of utmost importance. Trusting in something bigger and trusting in you is the only way to live. Everything will work out the way that it is supposed to, if only you have faith. I thought about suffering, a lot. I cried when I thought of a life filled with suffering, whether that life is a human life, an animal life, or any life.

Time became irrelevant. I had no concept of it. There was no yesterday and there was no tomorrow. I could hardly imagine going back to my "regular life," though I knew I would. I also realized that dreams are important. I couldn't figure out how or why but I got the feeling they were so important.

I thought a lot about people. I had encountered some truly inspirational people during my journey so far. I thought about particular people and what I had learned from them. I thought that maybe they were placed in my life for a reason. I felt as if each and every one of us has a unique purpose. I realized what a great love I have for people. I also thought about animals a lot. Years later I would be exposed to a world where animals were subject to lifetimes filled with suffering for nothing more than humanity's greed and mass-consumption. I was and would become even more passionate about the rights of animals. I saw beauty. Rather, I *felt* beauty. And I *felt* love. So much love.

As I came off the trip I continued to think. My body was exhausted. I had gone so many places and seen so much in less than a day. I had experienced so many emotions, truly *feeling* them, deep in my core. I felt divine, holy, and connected. This was the most spiritual experience of my life and I would be forever changed.

I would go on to have more experiences with magic mushrooms in my life, but this first experience was of such importance to me. It is so unbelievable that this earth has something so powerful that can show someone what is truly important. I had always had a faith in something, whatever that was. However, now there was absolutely no doubt in my mind that we were moving toward something big, connected to something nobody could fully understand. Ti told me about a bunch of other various plants with medicinal and hallucinogenic properties. The earth provides everything we need. There is so much to learn from nature.

I remember waking up the morning after eating the mushrooms feeling content and refreshed. I was myself, but I was slightly different, slightly better.

I lived with the natives a little while longer, becoming closer and closer to Ti everyday. I loved her and felt as if we had a bond that could never be broken. Through space and time, we would always be connected in some way.

When I finally left this village, I continued to make my way through the Amazon. The pink river dolphins, loud howler monkeys and gentle sloths kept me company on my journey. Everything looked a little more magical than it did before. I wanted to tell the world about the power of this fungus. But maybe the world wasn't ready for such a thing. Maybe it would unite everyone, but then again maybe it wouldn't. It wouldn't be long before I would encounter a people obsessed over a different "drug."

As I continued to think about my mushroom trip, I realized how unique it was to *me*. Everyone experiences something different and that is the beauty of it. No amount of words can fully explain such an experience. In order to truly understand, you have to personally *feel* it. There is a world of difference.

FIFTEEN

SWEET AND SINISTER

Barbados
~1710

I traveled through the Amazon for many years. Ti and her family gave me a canoe so that I could continue by way of the river. I often stopped, trekking into the green forest and living on the land until I felt ready to continue on my way. I loved the serenity of the jungle. I also loved having such a large flow of water to guide me in a direction. However, at times I missed the ocean. I was longing for the simplicity of island life again. However, I was here right now and I made sure I appreciated the beauty of such a diverse place.

I would go on to learn that the Amazon rainforest has unsurpassed biodiversity. The Amazon River and all of its streams and tributaries contains the largest number of freshwater fish species in the entire world. I recently heard that one in ten known species in the world lives in the Amazon rainforest! I could go on to write chapters just about the Amazon's intriguing diversity, but I will leave it at this: The Amazon is a spectacular place, serving as the lungs of the planet, teeming with answers to questions we have yet to uncover.

I had become much more aware as I trekked through the endless green jungle after departing from Ti and her tribe. The Amazon natives had opened my eyes to the dangers that lurked within this mysterious land. I experienced encounters with the black caimans, slithering anacondas, electric eels, fierce jaguars and cougars, intimidating piranhas and the various species of poison dart frogs. While I knew there were hazardous animals, I still had peace of mind, never really feeling threatened. I found that it is important to be aware, but it is important to keep a positive, calm mindset as well. My fascination with these amazing creatures overpowered any fear I may have had of them. As always, some days I had more energy than other days, but I had a newly found faith in the Universe. I trusted I was heading in the right direction. I encountered a few native tribes during my journey onward. I was lucky to never have any problems with any of them along the way. I guess I didn't look too threatening and the fact that I could always speak with them made everything much simpler.

Eventually, I reached the ocean. It felt as if I hadn't seen the sea in forever. I didn't waste any time diving right in. I was ready to be a mermaid again. I was excited to explore the Caribbean Sea. As I traveled through the water, I appreciated every minute. I loved how the rippling waves glistened under the moon, I loved swimming through the clear blue hues of the ocean and I loved the smell of salt in the air. The islands in the Caribbean were tropical and lush. I sensed that a new phase of adventure was awaiting me.

The strong wind gave me an energetic feeling as I reached my first stop on the Caribbean island of Bonaire. The island was small, beautiful and lively. The Dutch had colonized the island but there were many African slaves living on the island as well. I stayed enough of a distance away, observing the people but mostly exploring as much of the natural beauty as I could without being seen. I would continue along hopping from island to island, swimming through the shining sea, and basking in the vibrant sun, loving life and this beautiful planet. I was feeling bold and unstoppable as I traveled through the Caribbean.

I was always wary of pirates, as they were plentiful in the Caribbean at that time. While pirates were gnarly and often unforgiving, something about their lifestyle intrigued me. Rather than choose a secure life on shore, living by the laws of the land and their (sometimes) corrupt governments, these men chose a different path. Life at sea was anything but easy. Rough waters, threatening enemies and instability made for many unknowns.

Yet, these men were living in the moment, forced to see whatever good happened upon them. In a sense, I felt thrilled and inspired by the lives of these sea dogs. Commoners feared them, but they enthralled me. Sometimes I would watch a ship full of pirates make their way through the dark night, looking for the next place to dock. I observed the way they drank tons of rum, many times playing rough, but still laughing and living. Some were more "moral" than others, but they were people just like anyone else. I had found that everyone had a light and dark side. It's just that some people had more of a light about them and others had more of darkness. I also saw that people's light would fluctuate from time to time, often dimming in times of sadness or brightening up in times of happiness. Some people lost a lot of their childhood light as life broke them down, while others were bright and vibrant throughout their lives. People truly amazed me. Many people have told me I only see the good in people. However, I truly believe there is something good to be seen in everyone, even if the bad outweighs the good, there is always a light no matter how dim it may be.

These thoughts would be tried as I made my way from Bonaire to Isla Margarita to Grenada to Tobago and eventually to Barbados, where I would settle for some time. Barbados was a paradise. As I approached the island, I felt as if there was something special about this place. It was a lovely and simple island. Stories that William had told me back when we had known each other in the Galapagos flooded my memory. He had explored deep into the Caribbean and I was excited to learn more about the stunning island of Barbados. However, it wasn't long before I realized the extent of exploitation happening on the beautiful land. Mostly enslaved blacks that had been brought in from Africa inhabited the island. I didn't truly understand what was going on until I befriended Katey.

Katey was a slave working on a sugar plantation in Barbados. She had two children who also worked on the plantation. She was sweet, but one could easily see that life had beaten her down. It took her awhile to open up to me. She was nervous around me upon our initial meeting. There was something special about her, something that drew me to her. She was a very pretty woman. She had smooth skin and long dark hair. Hard work was starting to age her, but I can imagine she still got a lot of attention from the local men. What I found most interesting about her was her mind. She was smart. She was really smart, but she was treated as if she was nothing.

In Barbados by 1700, there were over three times more enslaved blacks than there were free whites. The black slaves were there to cultivate sugar cane. As I got to know Katey and hear her stories, I became more engrossed with humans. How could one group of people control another group with such force and cruelty? The worst part was, the "civilized" whites were operating such a large-scale slave trade to feed their *addiction* to sugar!

Sugar is by no means essential to anyone's health. To watch not only a group of people exploited, but also a land exploited for a people living half a world away, made no sense to me whatsoever. Greed and power had gotten the best of the people living so luxuriously in Europe.

The sugar plantations required a great deal of backbreaking labor. African workers were forced into this work and then controlled through numerous slave codes that were developed throughout the years. So much land was devoted to sugar that a majority of food had to be imported from New England.

Katey opened up to me with time. She was a woman who believed in creating the best possible life for oneself despite one's circumstances. She had acquired quite a few books that she spent her time reading. She told me that she made sure to teach her children the importance of reading and gaining as much knowledge as possible. Katey had class. She had a lot of respect for herself. I really admired what a great mom Katey was. Her world consisted of her children. She would do anything for them. She devoted her life to raising her children and made sure to instill important values in them. I remember her telling me that she wanted her daughter to grow up to respect herself and her body. She made sure her daughter understood that women who respect themselves attract men that will respect them too. She also made sure her son understood that all girls are special and that he should always treat females with respect. Katey was strong minded and I know her children would grow up to make their mom proud.

As I got to know Katey, I became more and more angered by the actions of the Europeans suppressing them. I had seen suppression take place between all kinds of different people. I have never been one to think "the whites" or "the blacks" or "the Asians" or any particular "group" is at fault. People are people. But a people with power and money are often the group that controls and suppresses whatever other group has less money and power, regardless of race or religion. I also want to get a particular point across. Not *everyone* is at fault; rather a few in power are often the ones to blame. Most people live their lives getting by in whatever way they can, without really doing a great deal to change the system currently in place. At the point in time I had reached the Caribbean, it happened to be that the mostly West Africans were being suppressed by people from Western Europe (or rather the governments of these European countries).

It really disheartened me as I heard stories of how the West Africans came to be captives working on these sugar planta-tions. Katey told me about how many were kidnapped, while others were tricked into the slave trade. The story that nudged at something deep inside me is the one she told me about a particular countryman she knew many years ago. The countryman befriended a trader who invited him for dinner and then offered to show the countryman the ship lying on the river. The trusting countryman followed the trader to the small canoe that would row them over to the ship. The countryman was excited and awed by the huge ship. Little did he know that a bunch of other traders were waiting to jump on board the canoe to seize the countryman and drag him aboard the ship to await a life of slavery. Katey's stories haunted me. They sounded like nightmares. How could one person do such a thing to another? At what point does someone say "no, I won't be a part of that?"

I also frequently thought about the Europeans living their lives across the sea, sipping their sweet drinks, gossiping about the neighbors. Did they realize what was happening in the Caribbean so that they could indulge themselves in the addicting sweetness? I am certain most had no idea. Was it their responsibility to find out about these issues? My mind was filled with questions that I myself couldn't even find the answers to. I didn't know if my longevity and ease of travel was a blessing or a curse. There were times I wanted to stay deep out in the middle of the sea, in a bubble of a world, where I didn't have to see such destruction amongst humans. Why would I want to be exposed to so much cruelty? However, at the same time, my eyes were constantly opened to the good and bad sides of human nature. And yes, while there was a lot of bad, there was also a lot of good.

My time spent in the Caribbean really opened my eyes to a darkness I couldn't shake. I knew that Katey was destined to a life of enslavement, as were her children. It was hopeless and depressing to be quite honest. I wished there was something I could do to help. I knew in my heart that eventually, good would overcome the evil taking place right now, but that wouldn't save Katey or anyone else being tortured at the moment.

I had seen enough evil taking place in the Caribbean and I was ready to move on. I was hoping the next leg of my journey would show me some light. I thought back on my experience in the Amazon with Ti and the mushrooms. I tried to keep my trust in the good of something higher, but it was difficult to be so positive after all I had seen. With a tear in my eye, I left Katey behind, wondering if she would ever know freedom. I felt lucky to have been born as Annala, something I had never really thought of until now. In a sense, Katey's doomed life made me appreciate all that I had. Maybe everyone needs to see a bit of evil to truly understand the importance of feeling lucky. The funny thing is, even Katey often expressed to me how lucky she felt. She felt lucky to still have her health, her children, and the blue sky above her head. If Katey can feel lucky, I think anyone can.

SIXTEEN

NEAR DEATH

Antarctica
~1780

O nce I left the island of Barbados, I decided to head south. I kept thinking about what I saw on the islands of the Caribbean. There was definitely a lot of exploitation happening. And that would certainly not be the last time I saw a land and a people exploited.

I also thought a lot about the psychedelic mushrooms I ate in the Amazon as well as the sugarcane that was being cultivated in the Caribbean. Way in the future, I would see societies that shunned psychedelic mushrooms, weed, alcohol, and other "drugs." It was funny because sugar was the most addictive drug of all based on my recent experience on the Caribbean islands. It was also the most destructive to society. It is interesting how narrow-minded people can be.

I continued on my journey, without a real plan, as usual. I wasn't ready to hit land again just yet. I had seen the dark side of human nature and I wanted to spend enough time in the sea to cleanse my soul. Swimming my way through the ocean always left me feeling inspired and light again. It felt necessary for me to go back out to sea every so often, just to rejuvenate. The sea is comforting to me, but it is also an important part of who I am. While I may mimic a human on land, I have another side that needs to be acknowledged as well. Now at sea, I felt myself again.

There wasn't much I needed or cared about. The only thing that felt extra special to me was the shell ring I had found hundreds of years ago, back in the South Pacific. I truly cherished this piece of jewelry that seemed as if it was made for me. People constantly asked me about it, and it felt like a part of me in a sense. I even started having dreams about my shell ring. I worried about losing it. I felt anxious that it might break or fall off. I almost felt as if it defined me, and there was nothing else in the world that was as valuable to me as that ring.

I spent a long time traveling through the deep blue ocean, thinking, learning and discovering. The further south I went, the more distanced I felt from the societies humans had created on all the bodies of lands. I didn't know how long I had been traveling for because days at sea can easily turn into months, years and decades. However, as I went further and further south, I eventually reached a very different kind of desert than I had ever seen before. The cold air chilled my bones as I swam closer and closer toward the continent of Antarctica. This was the first land I would step foot on after ages spent in the water.

Antarctica is the driest, windiest and coldest continent. This isolated terrain was unlike any other body of land I had ever seen. The dreary, dreamlike desert of ice chilled me to the bone. My body differs from most humans in that I can easily adapt to various climates. I can survive much longer than humans can in extreme heat or cold. However, the air here was frosty and uncomfortable to say the least. I didn't know what to make of this place. I wondered if anybody lived here. I set to find out.

As I walked through this kingdom of ice, the majestic, frosted mountains, glistening icicles, crisp caves and shades of blue and white left me in wonderment. This land was unreal. It is hard to put in words what it was like to walk across this land, by myself, with nothing but vast, frigid, icy terrain surrounding me. I encountered penguins, seals, a few various plants and algae, but not much else. I traveled by land as well as by water around the huge body of land. I also spent time exploring the icy islands surrounding the mainland. There were absolutely no traces of humans anywhere. Had humans ever set foot on this land? Was I the first to discover this icy terrain?

I continued to travel far and wide, in awe. However, I started to get lonely after a while. The curious seals and comical penguins kept me company, but the dreary land was affecting my emotions.

I was longing for human interaction. Memories of past lands and people occupied my mind. I dreamed of Cosimo and the Renaissance. I wanted to wake back up in Florence in the arms of the man I once cared for so deeply. I thought about William Dampier and his unique take on adventure. I wanted to see him walking along the shore of our island in the Galapagos before the rising sun, anxious to meet me at our secret spot. I longed for a love I had yet to find.

I shivered as a cold breeze caressed my skin and I wondered where all the souls I had met along the way were at this very moment. When you spend a lot of time alone, I find that you have a lot of time to think. You start to doubt yourself yet trust yourself at the same time. You experience such a range of emotions as you tumble along on your journey. Here I was, in this freezing, desolate land, with nothing to do but keep moving along, thinking, exploring and discovering.

When I reached the Transantarctic Mountain range that divides East Antarctica from West Antarctica, the breathless beauty towering above my eyes blew me away. The intimidating range put me in a predicament. I was on the east side of the mountain range, and I wasn't quite sure how long the Transantarctic Mountain range was, but it looked as if there was no getting around it. Should I attempt to climb it? I would later find out that this mountain range is one of the longest on earth, stretching from the Ross Sea to the Weddell Sea, dividing Antarctica in half. With doubt, I decided to climb the towering rocks of ice. I started my ascent on a bright morning as the rising sun lit the sky with florescent pinks and yellows. As the morning turned to afternoon, I felt as if I was making good progress. I was feeling powerful and unstoppable as I gained height. I looked down below and was amazed at how far I had come in such a short amount of time. However, when I looked up, I saw that

I was nowhere near the top. Yet I knew I had to keep going. There was no point in turning back now. A few days went by. Everyday I was making progress, getting closer to the blue sky above my head. It was tough. The cold air frosted and dried my body, yet I still felt the sun burning my skin through the chilly breeze. Though the journey up was difficult, I felt immortal. I became too confident in my ability to keep moving up, and felt as if I could do anything. I was tried on the fourth evening of my upward climb. The sun would be setting soon and I knew that I would have to stop for the night, however, I decided to keep moving just a bit more before calling it a night.

The clouds above picked up some purple hues and the bright sky turned a bit darker. I wanted to reach a good resting point before the stars came out. I took a step forward when all of a sudden I saw a huge flow of ice and snow approaching from right above me. It all happened so fast. I don't know what triggered the avalanche, but in a matter of minutes, I was completely overtaken by loads of snow. In the seconds before getting covered, I was scared. I wasn't ready for death. I guess nobody ever is. No matter how much time you have, you always want more. I may have been living thousands of years, and even that wasn't enough.

The next hours are extremely difficult for me to describe. I felt as if I died. My body was buried beneath the snow, but my mind was elsewhere. First, I saw myself stiff and covered by the big slab of white powdery earth. I was looking down and I could see the dangerous terrain just ahead of where my body was. The mountain range was even bigger and longer than I had imagined. Then, I got this strange feeling as if something was trying to talk to me. I don't know who they were (or are), but they let me know that my time on earth was not finished yet. I saw darkness and beauty, good and evil, love and hate. I was taken to a place of light and I was shown a world that we cannot see, but that we are all a part of. And then, I was brought back to earth. I awoke, no longer covered by snow. My body was cold and weak. I was disoriented. The sun was bright and the ice around me was melted. It took me a few minutes to remember where I was and what I was doing. Then it all came back to me. Last I remembered, nightfall was approaching and an avalanche had taken over me. Did I spend the night covered in the ice? How did I get out? Did the sun melt it away? Where did I go last night?

I could barely get up. A range of emotions took over me. I knew that I had experienced something unreal. My near death experience was otherworldly. I felt so strongly now that I had some sort of purpose here and that I needed to continue on my journey. While I didn't know exactly what that was, I knew I had to trust in the Universe. I was overwhelmed with the idea that this earth is not all there is for us. There is something so much bigger out there and we are all a part of it.

I looked up at the even more intimidating range above me now and didn't know what to do. My weakened body would not be able to handle the rough terrain ahead. I debated going forward, but something told me to go back. I didn't want to "give up," but going back down seemed to be the best idea right now. It would be hard to climb down, but the endless journey upward would be nearly impossible.

I started my journey back the way I came. I knew it would take me awhile, but it was the only option right now. The next few days were dreadful. I was cold, weak, and unable to really recuperate. I kept thinking about what happened, not just the actual avalanche, but what happened when I was buried under the snow. Why did I experience such a spiritual revelation? Did I actually see what I saw? Or was everything made up in my head? As I thought more about it, I realized none of it could just be made up. The series of events was too unlikely to just have been a figment of my imagination. The other beings that showed me what I saw were very real. None of it made sense, but then again, this crazy world doesn't make sense either. Similar to my mushroom experience, I had a newfound faith. I realized that death is not something to fear. When you lose your fear of dying, it is only then that you can finally start living.

I finally reached the bottom of the mountain range. I didn't know exactly what to do now, but I followed along the edge of the towering mountains heading south. Eventually, I reached the Ross Sea. My eyes filled with tears when I saw the Southern Ocean. I was home. And I was alive.

SEVENTEEN

ROMANCE & CANNIBALISM

New Zealand
~1810

L eaving Antarctica was strange. This land was cold, desolate, and somber. Yet it was also dreamy, intriguing, and magnetic. On my final day on the icy wonderland, I decided to sit on the edge by the ocean, just observing the captivating land around me, waiting patiently, until the sun went down. I watched the clouds catch pinks and purples and I watched slabs of ice shift and fall. Each direction I looked, the sky and landscape looked unique and magical. To the east, the sky looked dark and stormy. I focused my eyes on the big white fluffy cloud to the south that was slowly picking up light pink hues with the bright baby blue backdrop. Dark purple, wispy clouds started to form around the giant white clouds. The setting sun in the west was peeking out from behind dark blue elongated clouds. There were rays illuminating the surrounding world. I closed my eyes for a few moments before opening them up to the fast changing sky. I looked up and saw that a rainbow had formed right above me. I got emotional over all the beauty I was taking in. Eventually, I watched the first stars appear in the sky. I would start my onward journey in the dark hours of the night. I don't know why, but leaving Antarctica wasn't easy. It was a darkly magical place that had truly moved me. This land was unreal and I wondered if I would ever return. I often wonder about that when I leave a place. There is always a chance, a good chance, I will never return. It is a strange thing to think about.

The moon was a waning crescent, big and bright in the sky as I entered the ocean to swim my way to wherever I was going. I could see the outline of the rest of the circular moon, surrounding the bright yellow, sliver of a crescent, mesmerizing me as I floated away from Antarctica. I swam for a while. When I am in the ocean, time seems to be irrelevant. I have no concept of it as I swim endlessly through the deep blue sea.

Eventually, I reached the South Island of New Zealand. The land looked like a place one can only think up in their imagination. I waded up to the southern part of the island, from the Tasman Sea, and nervously looked up at the jagged coastline revealing a land that would open up my world to a whole other "there." I spent so much time traveling through the hills, bathing in the rivers, and eventually reaching the Southern Alps. My body worked hard as I forced it up and down mountains without taking much of a break. I then worked my way toward the east coast where the land changed from mountains to hills to large coastal plains. I adored the creatures that inhabited the island, especially all the different birds that sang to me as I walked by myself through the bewitched land. Many of the beautiful birds I spent so much time listening to on the island have since become extinct. What most amazed me were all the landscapes this island offered. There was never a dull view, whether I was looking at fjords and glaciers, standing atop a lofty mountain or strolling through the sweeping plains. The contrasting scenery made for a hauntingly beautiful terrain. When I reached the top of the South Island, I swam my way up to the North Island.

I was feeling inspired after my travels through the heart-stirring South Island, but I was also feeling lonesome. It had been too long since I had interacted with any humans. I longed for human touch.

It was a starry night when I came across the Maori tribe that would become the human interaction I was looking for. The Maori people had been living on both the North and South Islands for hundreds of years. This particular tribe dwelled on the east coast of the North Island. As always, I was wary when approaching this new group, but was warmly welcomed despite the hostile references some have recorded of the Maori people.

The Maori people were very interesting to me. They lived simply, much like the other natives I had encountered on my journeys throughout the world. However, they had a lot of different aspects to their culture that took some getting used to for me. The Maori people were a people that took pride in their strength and warfare. Fighting was in their nature and the men were glorified for their strength and battle accomplishments.

Tane taught me a lot about his people and way of life. Tane was the chief's son. He was young, charming, strong and intelligent. I was drawn to Tane's fierce nature. Tane was highly revered amongst his people and I was surprised by the fact that Tane seemed interested in getting to know me. When I happened upon his people, I must have looked lost and lonesome. It had been a long time since I had interacted with anyone and I was ecstatic to have a people take me in and show me how they lived. Everywhere I go, people live with different rules and customs. It is always so interesting to me to learn about different cultures.

Most of all, I have learned that there really is no normal or correct way to live in this ever-changing world.

I remember the first time Tane spoke to me. I had heard other young girls in the tribe speak highly of him. He was a ladies man, always flirting with different girls and sometimes giving off an arrogant vibe. On a gloomy afternoon, I was startled when Tane came over to me and addressed me as "Anahera." I looked at him and smiled before correcting him on my name. He smiled and said, "I like Anahera more. It suits you." I must have looked confused because he proceeded by telling me a little bit more about my new name. "Anahera means angel." I couldn't help but smile a bit before asking him why that name suited me. "You are angelic in every way. You exude innocence and radiate purity. Plus, Anahera is similar enough to Annala. Think of Anahera as your nickname from me." He smiled and walked away. It was an interesting first interaction that left a lasting impression.

From then on, Tane would randomly come over and start conversations with me. I was always confident but slightly shy around him. I knew he flirted with many of the other girls and I didn't want him to think I was going to give him the attention he was used to. However, I was always friendly and I always enjoyed our banter. I came to find out Tane meant "man," which suited him well. Tane was the ideal image of a man in the Maori society.

I became close with many of the people in the tribe. We would sit around a fire at night, talking, eating and telling stories. The men were raised to prepare for battle from a young age. These people spoke of other tribes and ways of surprise attacking them. The Maori tribes seemed to be in never-ending battles with one another, but that was a part of their culture. While the Maori people were primitive and intense when it came to battle, to me, they were less barbaric than some of the "more advanced" cultures that went to war and left thousands of young innocent men for dead. In the Maori culture, it was common for a chief to fight one on one against another chief. The winner would bask in the fame that came along with the triumph. The one thing that took me some time to digest (literally) was the fact that the Maori people often ate the people they conquered. It was not unlikely for a Maori tribe to eat their recently defeated enemies while away from home during a battle.

Despite the fact that it was a little bit hard to wrap my head around the practice of cannibalism considering I often felt bad eating an animal, I got used to the Maori customs. Like I said, there is no real normal way of living. This is what the Maori did and it was an accepted custom amongst *all* the Maori tribes.

Tane and I continued to talk here and there, flirting a bit but never really spending too much time together one on one. Amongst the tribe there was mention of an upcoming fight. I would soon find out that Tane would be fighting another soon-to-be chief of a different local tribe. Tane would need to prepare for his future life or death scenario. With such an unknown future ahead, Tane and I started to talk more frequently and have deeper conversations. One night, when the moon was high in the sky and the bright stars were illuminated in the blackness surrounding, Tane and I sat up, long past the rest who had gone to sleep, by a dying fire, inching closer and closer to one another. Tane and I joked around a bit, but when he started to open up to me, I felt so much closer to him. He expressed his concern over the upcoming fight, despite the cocky air he usually radiated. He also told me that he had a secret that he was somewhat embarrassed by but wanted to tell me. I of course listened, curious as to what he might say. He proceeded to tell me that he only had one testicle. It was something he was very self-conscious about. I listened as he continued to speak, somewhat nervously about his situation. I told him that it wasn't something to be ashamed of. In fact, it made him unique. I was tempted to tell him about my fin, but refrained. I couldn't help but feel special that he trusted and wanted to confide in me. It also made me realize that despite the fact that so many people viewed him as the perfect man, even someone as "perfect" as Tane had flaws and insecurities.

Our conversation continued but the topics changed as the moon moved across the sky. Eventually, with only a few hours of darkness left, Tane leaned in to kiss me. At first I teased him as I rubbed my nose against his, playfully rejecting his kiss. However, after a few minutes of resistance, right when he was about to give up, I allowed him to kiss me. We kissed passionately, and continued to kiss passionately for what seemed like forever. I didn't want to stop kissing him, but soon enough the sky started to brighten and the birds started to chirp. A new day had arrived whisking away the dreamy night before.

To tell you the truth, I didn't know what to make of my steamy night with Tane. Did he really like me? Or was I another conquest? Only time would tell. Skeptical, I would let him come to me if he wished. Sure enough, Tane continued to make an effort to get to know me. So we continued to stay up together, late into the night, kissing under the stars. Neither of us wanted the other tribe members to know about our secret romance, so we kept it between us two. The secrecy made it more fun. During gatherings, Tane and I would sneak away to kiss behind the Kauri trees. It was thrilling having a fling with this man who held so much power amongst his people. Eventually, a few of our closest friends caught on to our romance, but they were good about keeping it a secret as well. While Tane and I were very different in many ways, he always treated me well and we truly enjoyed each other's company. He was much more obsessed over battle and status, while I was less impressed by symbols of status or war triumphs. However, he treated me like the angel he thought I was, and I felt loved and adored by him.

As time went by, we both knew his upcoming battle was right around the corner. Becoming more involved with Tane, I started to get anxious knowing the battle meant life or death for him. While I never thought Tane was a man I could spend an eternity with, I cared for him deeply, falling harder for him as so many uncertainties intensified our feelings.

In the days before the battle, I couldn't sleep. Emotions overwhelmed me as I imagined the battle over and over again in my head. Tane had been working hard to ensure he was at optimal strength, but I was sure his opponent had been doing the same. Tane tried to reassure me he would be fine, but nothing could calm my nerves.

The day of the battle was unbearable for me. Tane adorned his body with all kinds of various war paints and tattoos. In the nights before, the entire tribe engaged in ceremonies and dances in the hopes of bringing on a successful fight. I didn't want him to fight. I thought it was petty to continue fighting battles against people because of "tradition." However, in the moments before battle, Tane sat me down and told me, "Anahera, this is what we do. This is what we have done for generations. Fighting is a necessary evil. If I didn't engage in this battle, sooner or later, my men would and I would engage in a different battle. We all live and we all die. I can say that I am proud of the life I have lived thus far, and I hope that this is not the end, but if it is, that is okay. I am so glad to have met you Anahera. You have filled voids in my life with your heavenly presence. You are my angel." I started to cry as I hugged him, hoping this would not be the last time I hugged him. I didn't want to let go.

The day went by and I sat inside my hut, thinking about Tane. I respected the courage it took for him to fight. I thought a lot about what he had said to me earlier. The fact that he was fighting his own battle meant much more than the rulers who sent out the poor to fight battles on their behalf, as had been customary for many other cultures. However, I couldn't get the knots out of my stomach that day. I was driving myself crazy. I even thought about leaving and returning to the sea so that I wouldn't have to face the potentially devastating news. Maybe not knowing was better than knowing a bad end result...

However, I knew that I had to stay. I couldn't live my life wondering if he came back. And if he did come back, what would he think if I had left? So I waited. And waited. How could so much time pass by at sea and I didn't know where it went, but now, this one day, felt like forever? The dawn sky crept in and news came. Tane was the talk of the town. He had beaten his opponent. It was a tough battle but Tane made it out alive. The relief I felt was unlike anything I had ever experienced before.

When I finally saw Tane, it felt like ages had passed since I had last seen him. His body was covered with scrapes and bruises but that didn't matter. He was alive! That night there would be a major celebration. The tribe would have a feast and engage in traditional ceremonies around the latest win.

Tane was like a celebrity. Everybody wanted to talk to him and hear about his experience. All I wanted to do was spend the night in his arms, away from the chaos. However, tonight was a big deal for him and everyone else. As was customary, the tribe would make a meal out of the man that Tane had just defeated. The enormous fire lit up the night. The smell of meat and cooked vegetables soon filled the air. When it came time to eat, I took a seat next to Tane. Everyone would get a taste of the enemy. I had a weird feeling about eating another human. I didn't know what I should do. Should I refuse? What would these people think if I rejected their custom? Would they regard me as the enemy? Is it wrong to eat a human? Is it any more wrong than eating an animal? Questions flooded my mind.

I sat around the fire, Tane by my side and took a bite. I chewed and swallowed.

Would eating humans become a normalcy for me? No. But eating animals on a regular basis would never be a normalcy for me either. The man I ate lived a life of freedom with the ability to choose whether or not he wanted to go to battle, with the ability to choose what he did with his time, with the ability to roam the land freely. That would be a choice many animals were not granted in the future of factory farming and mass consumption. However, that is a whole other topic. Is it wrong to eat another human being? Is that question even black and white? I couldn't give you an answer.

Tane would become a legend amongst his people. Stories of this epic battle would be passed on for generations. I was happy for him. However, with time, I got this nudging feeling that it was time for me to move onward with my journey. I was not meant to stay here forever and I knew that there was so much more out there for me to experience. Tane knew it too. I was sad to leave him but it was necessary. The time we spent together would never be forgotten. He was my man and I his angel.

EIGHTEEN

SEA OF BLOOD

Atlantic Ocean
~1850

After leaving New Zealand, I swam through the Indian Ocean tracing the outline of Africa into the Atlantic Ocean. With time I found myself back up along the coast of North America. A lot had happened since I left New Zealand but one thing I know is that I will never forget the day I saw a sea of blood that would change my life forever.

It was a beautiful day and I was in a good mood. I had spent the night before gazing up at the waxing crescent moon, my passion and spirits growing with the moon. It was early afternoon and the blue sky was filled with clouds of various shades and sizes coasting by peacefully.

I don't know what I noticed first, the majestic humpback whale or the large ship in the distance. Seeing this whale so close brought back memories from a long time ago. I was eager to get closer. As I approached the humpback, it released a stream of liquid through its spout. I was in a dreamy daze as emotions came over me bringing me back to the time I spent with my long-lost friend. I felt a deep connection to this giant, peaceful creature. I heard yelling in the distance. I perked my head up to get a clearer sound of a man singing out, "There she blows!" He repeated this multiple times before I saw the men launching smaller boats into the water.

From the moment the boats were launched in the water, the crewmembers seemed to be in a hurry to reach the whale, while still trying to be as silent as possible. I watched all the while, confused and curious as to what these men wanted. I was there in the water, observing. Looking back, I am surprised nobody noticed me sooner considering I was not focused on staying hidden. I guess the men were so concentrated on the large animal that they failed to see me. Once they were within a few feet of the whale, I heard a man yell "give it to him!" Right then, the harpooner plunged his barbed weapon right into the back of the whale. I panicked and screamed. The men were so caught up in the moment they still didn't notice me. Why were these men trying to kill the whale? I didn't see it do anything to them. The whale thrashed in pain as the boat backed away. I heard the men screaming "Stern all! Stern all, for your lives!" I quickly swam closer to the whale but immediately backed away as I watched the whale dive down, fighting for its life. The crewmembers were scared, I could tell. I would be too. This was no easy task, killing this enormous, powerful animal. Soon enough the whale needed to come back up for air. The boat was tugged along as the whale sped through the water. I followed from behind. Finally, the whale got tired. I watched as the men pulled on the line to draw their boat closer to their prey as some of the men switched places in the boat. Everything was happening so fast, but right now, it was nearing the end. The boatheader lunged a lance into the lungs of the whale. I watched the dying creature spout blood with every breath.

I started to cry and as the boat backed away, I moved forward. I went right over to the whale without a care as to who saw me. The first drop of blood spewed onto my skin and touched me in a way I can't describe. I sobbed as I swam over to the whale. It was swimming frantically in circles, until eventually it came to a stop. It no longer had the energy. I got closer and touched its body as it slowly lost its life. I looked into its eyes, feeling as if I was once again looking into the eyes of my friend I once knew so well. The whale looked back at me. To this day, I hope my eyes expressed sympathy and love in its last living moments. This was the end. The whale turned over on its side. The men now had to tow the whale back to the ship. Right before the exhausted men started their laborious work back to their ship, a man noticed me and pointed me out to the crew. They stared, dumbfounded at the sorrowful mermaid staring back at them. I hope they felt remorse as tears flooded my eyes, filling the sea with unwanted salt water. By this point it was nearing night, the sky filled with fluorescent pinks and yellows. I stared deep into their souls before diving down into the red sea.

In the next couple of days I watched as the men processed the carcass. Sharks had come to feast and the men tried to work as quickly as possible. By the end, even after I watched the crew clean up the blood and oil soaked boat, the odor emanating from the ship was unbearable.

At this time in history, so many whales were slaughtered for lamp oil, animal feed, soaps, cooking oil and corsets. Whaling was at an all-time peak. Many species neared extinction. As I thought more about the mass killing of a species, I wondered whether it is the responsibility of humans to be stewards of the environment. I know that everything lives and everything dies, but it seems wrong to kill a species in mass because of greed. Is it okay for humans to take as much as they want with no regard for the environment or the animals they are slaughtering? At some point species after species will go extinct. What will humans do then? In the 1700's and 1800's alone, countless species went extinct because of humans. Some of these include Steller's sea Cow, the Sardinian Pika, the Bluebuck, the Great Auk, the Atlas Bear, and the Eastern Elk, along with so many other species. However, as I write now, in 2015, it saddens me to think about how many more species have gone extinct solely because of human activity. The Passenger Pigeon, the Kenai Peninsula Wolf, the Bali Tiger, the Caspian Tiger, and the Eastern Cougar are just a few. Not only have tons of animal species reached extinction, but so many plant species as well. Every single day, countless species are lost due to habitat destruction, introduction of alien species to an environment, pollution and overexploitation.

I thought about the death of the whale I had just witnessed. Then I thought about how many more were being killed off every single day. It didn't seem sustainable. I will always have a powerful bond with whales and an urge to protect them. There is something so majestic and elegant about these giant animals that swim with grace through the ocean. Imagining an earth without them brought me to tears.

As I put my thoughts onto paper right now, in the year 2015, I can't help but think about all the species that are critically endangered. Some of these include, The Amur Leopard, the Black Rhino, the Mountain Gorilla, the Leatherback Turtle, the South China Tiger, the Sumatran Elephant, the Sumatran Orangutan, and so many more. The list goes on and on. I hope that by the time you are reading this, these animals have not since died off.

It seemed to me that so many people had become so disconnected from the natural environment around them. How could people have no regard for all the different living things that shared the earth with them? Did people on shore know what was going on at sea? Did they know that so many whales were being killed off to a point of near extinction? My mind was clouded with questions leaving me in a hopeless state. I had always felt at peace while swimming through the sea. It was my sanctuary. Yet, it seemed that humans were encroaching on these precious waters as if they owned them along with everything else. Once people realize this earth is not theirs alone, everything will be better off.

NINETEEN

MARK MY WORDS

America
1854 - 1889

I arrived in New York City on a sweltering summer's day. The feeling I got when I arrived in this bustling city was similar to the feeling I got when I arrived in Lin'an, China, many years ago. This was an exciting place. At this time, it was the busiest port in the world. What a place New York City was with immigrants from all over the world, living in one city all together! So many different cultures blended in a single location making up the famed melting pot. The city was unlike any place I had ever seen before. Ships, crowded streets, theatres, taverns, and an age of machinery gave me mixed emotions as I wandered in awe at the fast-changing city. I felt like I had been at sea for forever. I was now entering the Industrial Revolution and I didn't know what to think about it all.

I saw beauty, luxury and a city of hope. People came from all over the world to work in the booming city. But I also saw a city of dark alleys filled with crime and prostitution. I saw people searching for a better life only to find themselves in dirty, disease-filled slums, longing for a simple life away from so-called progress.

I settled in New York City for a little while. I had a love hate relationship with this place. I loved that I was able to meet so many different people in a city that was more tolerant and culturally diverse than many other cities. But I hated the corruption and slime that came along with such a place. I met people who were out to take advantage of you, people that wanted nothing more than your money and your soul. The world was changing quickly. I could feel it in the air and I could certainly see it in New York City. Transportation was easy with the Hudson River, Erie Canal and the recent invention of railroads. It was slowly becoming easier for people to get from one place to another, uniting the world in a way unimaginable before. This was all amazing to me. But I saw how money had so much control over people. People were caught up in the grind.

I took a job at an Irish tavern. There were tons of Irish immigrants living in New York City at this time and they liked to stick together. I was lucky enough to land a job serving at a saloon that was constantly busy. I didn't make a lot of money but there wasn't much that I needed. Surrounded by Irishmen regularly, I learned to love drinking almost as much as the Irish. I even started to pick up a wee bit of an Irish accent!

I became accustomed to people swearing, drinking and making inappropriate remarks on a regular basis. While I was always fairly pure minded, my naivety was vanishing as I spent more and more time in the city. I learned to watch my back. I encountered a good number of people with questionable intentions, teaching me more about human nature. However, I also came across a good number of inspiring people who taught me to keep my trust in humanity, always.

I remember the day that Samuel walked into the saloon I worked at. He was not Irish and he was quite young which made him stand out. I brought him a beer and noticed he had a notepad with him. I was drawn to Samuel and I struck up a conversation with him. I learned that he had recently moved to New York City from Hannibal, Missouri to work as a printer. I could tell he was curious about me as well. I told him a little bit about some of my travels and I could tell he was impressed. As we continued to speak I could tell he was very wise despite the fact that he was only an 18-year old boy. He had a curiosity about the world and was open to learning and experiencing everything he could. He left that night after a few beers but that wouldn't be the last time I saw him.

I continued to work nights at the tavern, observing the different people that came in. During my days I would walk around the city and check out all the different shops, often looking for a quiet place to write in my journal. Sometimes I missed having my own intimate spot away from the dreary concrete jungle just to take a nap under a tree and listen to birds chirp before bathing in a nearby stream. I missed being surrounded by nothing but nature. I guess other people felt the same way because there was talk of a big park to be built. The year before I arrived in New York City, more than 750 acres of land central to Manhattan Island were set aside to create the first landscaped public park in America! It would become known as Central Park.

Working at the Irish tavern was fun, but my hours were long and my nights were late. Sometimes during my shift I would take my break out in the alley behind the saloon, standing outside, thinking about the world and what we are all doing here. In the alley behind my saloon was a whorehouse. Some of the women would stand on the street smoking cigarettes, looking for their next customers. I always smiled at the girls and wondered what it would be like to live a life like theirs. I often listened to them talk to one another about the different men they slept with. I couldn't imagine giving my body to just anyone. I still hadn't had sex with anyone and I still wanted to wait to be in love. It seemed that so many people became so disconnected from their bodies. Sometimes I felt bad for the girls that felt as if they had no other choice than to sell their bodies to whoever was willing to pay. I saw some of the men that approached the women and I would never want to come as close as rubbing noses with some of them, let alone having sex with them. Life was hard for so many people.

Samuel started frequenting the Irish tavern, popping in to say hi every couple weeks or so. He would sit down to drink a couple of beers and converse with me about life. Sometimes when I got off work, I would join him for a beer, always enjoying our philosophical conversations. He always made me laugh with his many opinions about society and people. Samuel was sarcastic and witty. He was anti-religion having interacted with many religious people he thought to be hypocrites. He once said to me, "If Christ were here now there is one thing he would not be – a Christian." I thought long and hard about this comment. I couldn't help but agree with the fact that so many people I encountered on my travels who were supposedly religious were often the people who seemed to lack the most basic sense of morality. Would a man like Christ be disappointed if he knew how many people wronged others in his name?

Not too long after I developed some sort of schedule and routine in New York City, I met John. John was a good man who loved his country and loved a good time. He asked me out on a date which led to another date and then another until we were frequenting theatres, restaurants and strolling around New York City in our free time. I enjoyed John's company and he seemed to always want to see me, but I knew deep down, from the very beginning, that we were really different. While we could have fun together, there was something missing. There was a disconnect. John's family owned a tobacco plantation in Louisiana. John was a physician. He had moved away from Louisiana to work in New York City. He said he preferred city life to farm life.

I remember walking down the street with John on a chilly afternoon in November and seeing a shop sign that caught my eye. The sign was a simple one. The image featured was a whale. Above the body of the whale I read, "Soapine did it!" with a man standing besides the whale next to a bar of soap. I stopped to look at the sign and John looked confused. He could tell I was upset but didn't understand why. The whale product being advertised glorified the image of the whale. Did people understand what really happened out at sea in order for this product to sit so beautifully wrapped in whale décor in the shop window? I told him there was no need to hunt whales for the stupid products people think they need. He still looked confused and told me that the whaling industry provided us with products we otherwise wouldn't have. I tried to explain to him how intelligent whales are and told him that the mass killing of so many different types of whales wasn't worth anything we might gain from it. He didn't seem to understand me and I guess I didn't understand him either.

I would continue to notice advertisements featuring beautiful whale art on the signs promoting everything from umbrellas to corsets. I hated seeing these signs. Marketing can be so deceiving. I don't think people knew or cared about the ugly process behind these whale products.

One evening I was sitting with John at a nice Italian restaurant. He always treated me really well and I can't deny that I truly had fun with him. We spent a lot of time laughing together which I have found is always a good sign. However, there were too many differences between us that often made me question our relationship. That night at dinner, we were speaking about the country of America. He told me it was the greatest country in the world. I looked at him and smiled. It was a great place but I knew that John had never been to any other country. How could he be so sure America was the best? He always spoke about this land of opportunity and how people were coming from all over the world to pursue the "American Dream." He was right. People were coming from all over the world with the hopes of a better life. However, I had been around long enough to see many people living in many different places. Some people made it big in America, but many lived hard, grueling lives. Would an enslaved African American living on John's family's plantation agree that America was the best country in the world? Just 100 years ago there was no America. Was there a "best country" before America was founded? Is it even fair to say that there is a "best" country? Like everything else, countries are temporary. The imaginary borders we create are temporary.

The following night, Samuel came to visit me at work. When I finished up with work, I sat down to have a beer with him. I told him a little bit about my conversation with John the night before. Samuel laughed and said, "Well you know what I say about patriots right?" I smiled and told him I hadn't a clue. He proceeded, "Patriot: the person who can holler the loudest without knowing what he is hollering about." A huge grin crept across my face. He was right.

I stayed awhile in New York City. I grew to love so many things about the city. I even grew to love the dark alleys, smoke-filled bars, and the dirty old men with the most interesting stories. The city was terrifying and sensational at the same time.

But soon the time came for me to bid my Irish bar family goodbye and head south. Samuel had long since moved away, though I got the feeling we would cross paths again. Too many seasons had come and gone, making me antsy for an unknown adventure. It was exciting to be here, alive in a time when travel was becoming easier than ever before! I could hop on a train and be in another city in just a few days. There were so many amazing innovations happening that were changing the world.

I traveled throughout America for years and years, watching how changes were happening exponentially. I saw the good and evil that always seems to come along with progress. I experienced love and hate in so many different forms. I saw the wicked side of slavery, but I saw the people that devoted their lives to freedom. I saw people abused, animals abused, and land abused. But through all the bad, I promise there was still good. I came across so many different people during my travels, all with their very different opinions. There were people I wanted to hate because of their close-minded views, but couldn't. People can be so bad, but still have a tiny light, one that glows ever so dimly, allowing you to love them, even if just a very little bit. People are so complicated it's unbelievable. But people are people.

It was 1864 and I had made my way across the huge country of America and found myself in California. I made it to San Francisco. I very vividly remember the day I arrived in this city that I had explored so many years ago, right before my encounter with Captain Drake! Here I was again. Man, how things had changed. I felt almost lost being here. I didn't really know what to do upon my arrival. So I decided to check out a local saloon. Something about the bar crowd always comforted me. In a bar you never feel judged or looked down upon. No matter who you are, you can walk into a bar, order a beer and do as you please. Whether you wish to socialize, play a game of cards, or just sit by yourself in a corner, the choice is yours. I feel at home in a bar. Well on this particular evening, a chilly breeze in the air, a night of unknowns ahead, I walked into a San Francisco bar. I should have been shocked, but I wasn't. I should have known I would find Samuel sitting in the tavern. It was as if no time had passed. I pulled up a chair next to him and we started where we left off back in New York City.

Samuel had grown and changed quite a bit, I guess as had I. However, his physical appearance had changed significantly; whereas, he commented on the fact that I didn't look a day older than when we last saw each other. "It's all the beer I drink," I said as I winked at him. He looked at me curiously.

Samuel told me all about the adventures he had experienced in our time apart. He had become a licensed river pilot and told me about the time he spent on the Mississippi. Samuel really opened up to me that night- more so than he ever had before. As the alcohol flowed through him, he became more and more talkative. He became really emotional as he told me about his brother that was tragically killed in an explosion on the steamboat *Pennsylvania* at 20 years old. Samuel blamed himself being the one that convinced his brother Henry to train to become a steamboat pilot. To top it off, Samuel told me about the vivid dream he had about his brother dying just a month prior to the accident. He took it as a sign something was going to happen and would live his entire life with guilt. Samuel also spoke of his own death. He told me he would go out with Halley's comet, having come in with Halley's comet. I listened, intrigued by all he had to say. I felt a strong cosmic energy radiating from this man. I felt as if I had known him for eternity.

Samuel also told me about his new pen name. He had signed his latest travel account with "Mark Twain." His pen name referred to the river depth at which a boat is safe to navigate, a phrase he learned during his time spent on the Mississippi River. He was drunk now and so was I. We were having a grand old time, sharing stories about our American adventures. Samuel continued the discussion with our usual philosophical talk. I remember him picking up his now lukewarm beer, taking a sip and then looking at me before saying, "Annala, but who prays for Satan? Who in eighteen centuries has had the common humanity to pray for the one sinner that needed it most?" I laughed at the predictableness of his question. He was always so questioning of religion and I loved that about him. Those who question the current normalcies are the ones that shift this world.

He then looked at me with sleepy eyes and said, "Annala, you are a very special girl. Don't ever forget it. You are great. You know why? Because great people are those who make others feel as if they too, can become great." If that is true, which I think it is, then Samuel was a great guy. He would go on to change the world. Mark my words.

TWENTY

FEELINGS OF
BEAUTY & LOVE

Paris
1889-1891

When I left California, I headed back east, eventually entering the Gulf of Mexico. I swam through the Gulf of Mexico, happy to be back in the sea. I remember the day I encountered what must have been over 100 whale sharks all swimming together off the coast of Louisiana. I was amazed as I watched the huge aggregation look so serene. These fish, the largest in the world, grow to over 45 feet each! Though they are intimidatingly large, they are extremely peaceful. With all that I have seen, it is still hard to believe that there are so many beautiful creatures that roam this earth through the wet and the dry, and the hot and the cold.

I made my way back to Florida, venturing once again to where I lived many years ago with the Tequestas, reminiscing on my time with Apenimon and Sisika. This land had changed so much since I last saw it. I felt sad in a sense. I then headed north, back up to New York, traveling both by land and by sea, along the eastern coast of the United States. I reached New York in 1889 where I would travel across the Atlantic to Paris. However, this time around, I would travel across the Atlantic via a very different mode of transportation than I was used to.

It was a Wednesday in New York and I would soon be boarding the steamship that would transport me across the Atlantic Ocean. In a week I would be in Havre, on my way to Paris. For the first time in my life, I would not be swimming my way across the vast Atlantic. It was a strange feeling boarding the French steamship with so many other people excitedly chatting about Exposition Universelle. The boat was beautiful and luxurious. People could enjoy concerts, extravagant meals, and wine with dinner every night. Another pleasant feature was the "Captain's Dinner" which took place the night before our arrival. This farewell celebration was a joyous night of champagne, music, and opulent meals.

I remember watching all the different people board the ship, delighted about the journey ahead. The women were dressed in their finest attire, garnished with feathered hats and excessive amounts of luggage. I felt so plain in my simple dress and my modest bag. Yet, I was content with my minimal amount of baggage, feeling light and free. The only piece of jewelry I wore was my shell ring, sitting comfortably on my pinky. One thing I didn't understand (and never will understand) is why so many women care so much about beauty to a point of selfishness. As I watched woman after woman board the giant ship, I looked at the ornamental accessories on their heads. Each woman's hat seemed to be more extravagant than the next. What angered me most was the fact that these women's headwear was made from real plumage of beautiful birds that were being wiped out in staggering numbers. Retail stores on Manhattan's Ladies Mile sold the feathers of great blue herons, snowy egrets, and white ibises. There were women with entire stuffed owls on their heads and whole hummingbirds covered in jewels accessorizing their wardrobes. More than 5 million birds were being killed off yearly by 1886. The good news was that there were women who cared. For the first time in history there was an environmental movement starting. This first environmental movement was geared toward saving the birds, which comes as no surprise to me.

I have always loved birds. Throughout my travels I encountered so many beautiful birds that kept me company as I ventured through the land alone. Listening to them sing and looking at their lovely patterns and colors always made me feel safe and at peace. As long as birds were around, everything seemed okay. It was upsetting to see so many women mindlessly wearing these decadent hats, which looked ridiculous if you ask me. Charles Warner, the Audubon Society pioneer, put it perfectly when he claimed, "A dead bird does not help the appearance of an ugly woman, and a pretty woman needs no such adornment." I couldn't have said it better myself.

On the first night of our departure, I enjoyed a good meal and slept soundly in my cabin. I was not one of the rich women who enjoyed all the luxuries of first class travel, but I had more than I needed. The third night onboard I couldn't sleep. I decided to leave my cabin to go sit out on deck. I was the only one on deck, looking out over the railing feeling the strong breeze wisp my hair in every direction. I looked up at the starry sky and then back down at the black ocean. I had an urge to jump overboard and continue by way of the ocean, craving the salty sea on my skin. I thought about the excessive meals people gorged themselves in while gossiping to their so-called friends. I had met quite a few shallow women onboard whom I just couldn't relate to in any sense. I wondered why I felt so different than so many of these women. Was it because I was a mermaid? Did my brain work differently than a normal human brain? No. There were plenty of inspiring women who cared about more than just their collection of *things*. They were just harder to come across.

What I enjoyed most on my steamship journey was all the music I was able to listen to. I would sit listening to the bands play while writing in my journal or just watching the different people walk by. To me, music is so special. The blend of different people and instruments come together to form something magical. Certain songs touch you in such an intimate way it is hard to describe the emotions that accompany such sounds. The exorbitant meals were sensational at first, but after a couple of days I felt as if the excessive amounts of food were wasteful and unnecessary. I didn't see the point of such gluttony.

What amazed me most was the ease of travel. In just a week, anyone could now be across the world! With traveling becoming so easy, people from all over could be united. It was an incredible time to be alive. Little did I know the future of traveling would become easier and easier in the years to come.

We docked in Havre and I was excited to be on land again, heading to Paris! If there was ever a time to be in Paris, it was now!

It was summer of 1889 and talk of Exposition Universelle filled the air. People from all over the planet were making their way over to Paris for this world fair. That year was the greatest year of ocean travel known theretofore.

I arrived in Paris on a bright, warm Friday morning. I entered the fair through the newly built Eiffel Tower, the legacy of 1889. There was commotion all around- a good kind of commotion. I roamed around the Champ de Mars, the Trocadéro, the quai d'Orsay, the Seine, and the Invalides Esplanade, taking in everything happening around me. The exposition, celebrating the 100th anniversary of the storming of Bastille, was a fair of performances, unbelievable structures, music and attractions bringing in a blended crowd of people from all walks of life. The Eiffel tower and the Galerie des machines were two of the most significant structures built for the event. The Galerie des machines, an iron structure composed of hinged arches, was the longest interior structure in the world!

I spent days and days venturing around, taking in everything I could. As I made my way through different parts of the city I was able to enjoy Buffalo Bill and Annie Oakley's "Wild West Show," listen to Javanese gamelon music and Parisian opera, and taste so many different foods. Buffalo Bill's show gave Europeans a taste of a distinctly American exhibition. His show was packed when I watched it. It was amazing to see so many people enthralled by his portrayal of the American Wild West. People were genuinely interested in other cultures.

The music I heard during the exhibition in Paris opened up my ears to new and exciting tunes. There were so many different sounds traveling through the air, so many different aromas blending, coming and going, and so many different sights stirring the imagination. The exposition brought on a feeling of excitement, magic, and change.

Another main exhibition featured at Exposition Universelle was a Negro Village. The village was ultimately a human zoo featuring 400 people in their "native habitats." It was a strange thing to see people on display. It felt wrong to see these humans who were being spectated by others. It almost felt as if these people were being dehumanized, being viewed as falling somewhere in between animals and the "civilized" Europeans.

Soon enough, the summer ended. I started to spend less time in the crowded areas of the fair and more time figuring out what

I would do next. By October of 1889 I found a small apartment in Montmartre and took a job that would help pay the bills.

On October 6, 1889 the Moulin Rouge opened in the Jardin de Paris. I would be doing clerical work for the cabaret that would become the most fashionable and popular place in Paris. I was writing clips and articles promoting the stylish cabaret that stood for beauty and pleasure. I loved the job. The money was not great but I was able to practice my writing and attend the extravagant shows for free! The venue attracted all different kinds of people from all over the world. I had worked in quite a few taverns and bar atmospheres previous to my stay in Paris, so a place like this was right up my alley. As Joseph Oller and Charles Zidler, the founders of Moulin Rouge, got to know me and liked my work, they often asked me to help out with more than just the clerical work. During big events they would have me serve drinks and champagne to the elite guests. Not only was it fun being a part of such fanciful events, it was also a way for me to make good extra money. I became friends with many of the can-can dancers. All the girls loved helping dress me up, lending me sexy, elaborate attire for my nights on the floor. While I was never comfortable having all eyes on me, I became more comfortable being viewed as "sexy." I became accustomed to getting attention from the many drunken men that attended the shows and I learned to appreciate the attention, rather than feel awkward when a man hit on me. Yet, I felt as if many of the people I came across saw something more in me. Though men hit on me, most seemed to treat me with respect as well. I'd like to think I looked "classy" even in my bare, sexy cabaret attire. I think the way you view yourself inwardly has a lot to do with how people treat you. As I spent more nights on the floor, I came to love the cigar-smoke filled rooms, the smell of absinthe in the air, the loud upbeat music, the vibrant art and architecture, and the electric vibe that ran through the Moulin Rouge. It had soul. It was a sinfully alluring place and I was drawn to its dark and mysterious ambiance.

I think my favorite thing about the Moulin Rouge was the fact that people of assorted lifestyles mingled in this fashionably sleazy cabaret. The middle class, workers, polished women, businessmen, Place Blanche dwellers, foreigners, and artists alike came to lose themselves for the night. In a single spot, everyone could come to have a good time, regardless of who you were.

However, in a place where sex was abundant, I often found myself unable to relate to many of the women who were so free with their bodies. Many of the dancers no longer believed in love. They believed love would only last for so long, whereas, jewels and money were everlasting. I disagreed. I kept my belief that real love was the most important thing in life. In a world surrounded by people who seemed to have lost faith in the genuine connections between a man and a woman, I held on to my hopeful thoughts. While I differed from many of the people I worked with, everyone seemed to care about me and respect me. Though I think many of the girls found me to be naïve, they admired my zest for life. Little did they know I had been around longer than them. Just because I was positive, didn't mean I was naïve. But I let them think whatever they thought. They were living free lives as they pleased and so was I.

As I became close with the many different people who worked for the Moulin Rouge, I started to feel as if I had a family. Of course there were some people I was closer to than others, but overall I felt at home amongst these people I got to know so well. There was a head manager, Bruno, who started showing me some extra attention after I had been working for the Moulin Rouge for a little while. He was exceptionally smart, acting as the brains behind much of the operation. I had heard rumors of him being crazy about one of the can-can dancers. This particular dancer was nice in ways but had a big ego. She tended to brag and had an air of being better than the rest. She could also be rude, though I am sure her haughty nature stemmed from her own insecurities. She often opened up to me and she told me that Bruno was fond of her but that she didn't want anything to do with him. She mentioned having fooled around with him before but assured me it was a one-time thing. I listened and didn't think much of it since I wasn't hanging around Bruno regardless. I truthfully couldn't care less about who had relations with whom. There always seemed to be drama around different people sleeping together. I couldn't keep up and I felt as if none of it concerned me anyways. I was happy focusing on my writing, saving some money for my future endeavors and enjoying as much as I could.

As Bruno started to slowly try and spend more and more time with me, I wondered what was going through his head. Late one night, he walked me home after an evening of work at the Moulin Rouge. We had become more than coworkers, we were friends. However, when he tried to kiss me, I had mixed feelings. I resisted his kiss, not really knowing how I felt about him. I didn't know if it would be a good idea to kiss this man who was technically a manager to me, especially if I didn't even know if I wanted to date him. I playfully rejected Bruno's kiss, hoping work wouldn't be awkward in the following week. I told him I wasn't allowed to kiss him, being that he was my boss and all.

Time went by and Bruno would flirt with me every now and then but was always respectful and kind. Dating wasn't on my mind right now. It seemed as if Bruno liked me but I didn't know what I wanted.

One night I was hanging out at the Moulin Rouge, drinking some cocktails, conversing with some of my coworkers and frequent customers that I had become close with. Drinking was something I had grown to love over the years. I loved the buzz I got from a few drinks. I never drank to oblivion but the right amount of alcohol always put me in a convivial and playful mood. As I ran around the cabaret, talking to this person and that person, Bruno would pass by me every now and then and joke that he was going to come over that night. I flirted back, insinuating I would like him to come over. The alcohol was talking, but alcohol seems to speak the truth.

At one point in the night Bruno asked me to follow him up into the Jardin de Paris Elephant. In the garden there was a giant stucco elephant. On certain nights, men would be able to pay a franc in order to be entertained by a belly dancer inside the belly of the elephant, which served as an opium den. However on this particular night the elephant was empty. We walked up the spiral staircase located in the foot of the elephant and found ourselves in the luxurious, dimly lit den. Bruno sat down and motioned for me to sit on his lap. I did. I was extremely tipsy but I vividly remember kissing him for the first time in this forbidden place. If Oller or Zidler had walked in, we likely would have been in trouble. Yet neither of us cared. We continued kissing for a while but eventually Bruno had to get back down to the crowded venue. He couldn't be missing for too long before he would likely be needed somewhere. I went downstairs first and Bruno left a few minutes later to lock up. Bruno was one of the few people who had a key to the famed elephant den. We didn't want to be seen walking out of the lustful elephant together.

Right before I left that night I said goodbye to Bruno and told him I was going home. He still had to work a bit longer but he told me he would be at my place in an hour. I smiled and told him I would see him later. For some reason I didn't actually think he would show up. I had changed into my nightwear, wiped off all the makeup from my face and was about to get into bed when I heard a knock at the door. Bruno wasn't kidding.

I opened the door for Bruno and we went into my bedroom. We started kissing. In between our lips locking we laughed about our night of sneaking into the elephant. As things got steamier I felt the need to tell him I wasn't going to have sex with him. He replied, "I didn't ask you to have sex with me." I said, "I know, but I wanted to forewarn you." We kept kissing but soon enough I stopped him and said, "there's something I need to tell you." He paused anticipating what I was going to say. I came right out and told him I had never had sex with anyone before. He looked surprised and relieved at the same time. He later told me he thought I was going to break things off with him before they even got started. Me being a virgin was better news than that I guess. We fell asleep that night and I wondered where all of this would go.

To tell you the truth, I had fun kissing Bruno but I didn't think much more of it. I figured I would just see how it went. But Bruno was persistent. He wanted to see me often and eventually we were spending day after day together. He would plan adventures for us and I grew to really care about him. After just a few weeks he told me he loved me. We were lying in his bed, half asleep, when he first said it. I was surprised to hear him say it at first and yet I felt ready to say it back. I still hadn't slept with him and I still didn't know if I wanted to. For some reason, I had always held onto my virginity as if it was something special. And it was something special but the fact that I had waited so long made sex an even bigger deal. I had always wanted to wait to be truly in love with the person I first had sex with. I had heard many women tell me about their first times having sex. Many women referred to their first time as a regretful and painful experience. For me, I didn't want to regret it. I hoped it would be pleasurable and an act of love. While I had explored other forms of sex with other men in the past, I had never actually had intercourse before.

Bruno and I explored each other's bodies and minds, becoming closer to each other physically and mentally. He truly became my best friend. I felt as if I could tell him anything. I felt completely comfortable with him. He understood me and I understood him. There was a common intuition between us that is not always easy to find.

It was Friday, May 16, 1890. There was a big event at the Moulin Rouge that would be an all day affair. In the garden there were concerts, performances and all the alcohol you could consume. The weather was beautiful and I was excited to be able to mingle on this lovely day. I was "working" but I was also just there to drink and hang out. I was feeling alive and beautiful. As the alcohol flowed through my body, I found myself dancing with friends, hugging Zidler and looking deep into the eyes of Bruno. The night would be an early one for me since I was quite tipsy by 9pm. Bruno took me to his place where we started to kiss passionately. One thing led to another and it was becoming harder and harder to resist the temptation of sex. We came questionably close that night, but it wasn't until the morning after, on May 17th, that I finally decided the time was right. I woke up slightly hung-over next to a man I loved. For the first time in my life I experienced what so many people talk about, one of life's worshipped pleasures, sex. It was lovely. Not only was my first time pleasurable, it was with a man I loved. I got what I wanted and I was happy I waited.

Bruno and I decided to take a few days away from the city and head to the South to be near the sea. It had felt like a long time since I had been back in the ocean and I was excited to immerse myself in the sea. The sun was setting and Bruno and I left our stuff on the shore and decided to go for a swim. I took off my earrings and looked down at my treasured shell ring. I always kept my shell ring on me so I left it on my finger rather than leave it on shore with the rest of my stuff. I dove in, swimming through the salty water that felt so at home for me before making my way back to Bruno. I made sure I stayed "human" by keeping my legs, rather than allowing them to turn into a fin. It took some concentration considering my legs naturally want to change when they touch the salty sea. When I reached Bruno I wrapped myself around him and started to kiss him. As we kissed in the ocean, the sun going down, with nobody else around, we started to do more than just kiss. This would be only my second time ever having sex. As we started to get more physical with each other, I felt my beloved shell ring slowly slipping off my finger. This ring was the one object I had an attachment to. I felt as if it defined me in a sense. People still constantly asked me about it. It was unique. Before I could stop it, the ring slipped from my finger into the sand churned ocean, nowhere to be found. I had that shell for centuries. Bruno knew how much it meant to me. He stopped trying to seduce me to help me look for the ring, but I knew it was gone. I was upset but I was okay. I told him that we had to have sex now. It would make me feel better about losing the ring. It seemed pointless to lose it without finishing what we started. He smiled reluctantly, impressed at my calm composure. The waves were crashing. Bruno struggled to carry me up against the rough waves as he continued where we left off. As we had sex I looked up at the blue sky. The moon was new. I viewed the slivered crescent as a sign. It was a new beginning. It was a new phase of my life. My shell ring was gone, my virginity was gone and I felt free and surprisingly at peace. Nothing lasts forever.

Bruno and I would continue to date and become closer and closer as the days went by. We would take adventures together out into the forests of France and we would go outside of the city in the middle of the night to watch the stars come out. Bruno had recently taken up photography as a pastime. He would take pictures of the Moulin Rouge and enjoyed photographing some of the dancers. However once we started dating, he always wanted to take photos of me. We would venture out to a beautiful location and he would have me pose for him under the trees or out in a field as the sun went down. He quickly became an extremely talented photographer, often having some of his photos featured in local papers. I was even featured in some of his selected photos. His photos were artistic and different from what other photographers were currently doing.

Because Bruno was so intelligent, he always picked up on things easily. I was constantly impressed by the fact that he seemed to know everything. He knew so much about history, science, business, philosophy, and so many other topics. He also loved getting out in nature despite the fact that he worked in nightlife, at the busiest cabaret in all of Paris. He was passionate, kind, and adventurous. These were all qualities I found to be so attractive. He would stay up all night working at the Moulin Rouge and come pick me up as soon as he got off work, as the sun first started to light the sky so that we could go on an adventure together, regardless of the fact he didn't sleep. He wanted to spend time with me more than anything else and he made it evident. If a man loves you, he will never leave a doubt in your mind about it.

Bruno constantly told me I was the most beautiful girl in the world. While any man can say these words, I felt them to be true. He would look at me, without makeup on, my hair a mess and admire me in a way that felt so genuine. Beauty had become so important to so many women. Girls were constantly trying to out-do each other with more vibrant makeup, sexier clothing, and more elaborate hair-dos. However, I had found that no matter how many accessories and clothing a woman bought, none of that would contribute to her beauty. Beauty is not something that can be bought. Beauty is a feeling. I have always felt beautiful. However, that had less to do with my physical appearance than it did with my thoughts. I could see my reflection in the ocean waters, but the first time I saw myself in a mirror was back in Lin'an, China during the 1200's. Hua, my old friend, first showed me my reflection in the silver-mercury amalgam she used as a mirror. Nowadays, in Paris there were mirrors everywhere, especially in the dressing rooms of the Moulin Rouge. Women obsessed over their looks to a point of destruction. Feeling beautiful is important. If feeling beautiful entails putting on makeup, doing your hair, and dressing a certain way, then that is okay. I am never one to judge someone for doing something that makes them feel beautiful, unless it is at the expense of another human being, animal, or the environment. When you feel beautiful, other people see you as beautiful. Yet, it is not something that can be faked. It must come from deep within. However, I saw so many women selfishly obsessing over their looks, destroying the natural beauty that emanated from them.

I have had many women ask me if I ever worried about Bruno working at the Moulin Rouge. At first I was confused by that question. One woman expanded on the question by asking if I was ever nervous Bruno would succumb to the temptation of all the half-naked, beautiful women that surrounded him on a regular basis. To be honest, there was never a worry in my mind. I knew in my heart that Bruno loved me unconditionally. He loved me to a point that he would never want to ruin the genuine relationship we had. I was his best friend and he was mine. And through everything we were always honest with each other. If he was jealous upon seeing another man notice me, he always expressed it to me. We were open with one another and I believe that is the only way to be.

At this point in my life I felt completely and totally free. I felt free of any attachments and I was comfortable being myself. I thank Bruno for aiding me in the process of feeling free and at peace in my bare-naked form. There were points in time that society influenced me in regards to what I should look like or what I should wear. However, now in Paris, I learned to let go of what society regarded as "normal" when it came to fashion and body image. I felt beautiful. I felt physically beautiful because of something deep within. My soul felt beautiful. I also couldn't help but constantly admire all the beauty around me. The city of Paris was beautiful, even in it's foulest alleys and run-down edifices. The sunsets were beautiful every night and all the people living their very different lives were beautiful. In addition, I had found that there is no other way to live life than truthfully. First and foremost you must be true to yourself. If you are true to yourself, you will always be true to the people around you. A person that is open, honest and true will never live a tormented life. And in the end, what matters the most in this world, is love. Love this amazing planet, love the creatures that roam the earth and sea, love the people you are destined to cross paths with, and love yourself. There is nothing greater than love.

I felt a deep connection to Paris but my time there slowly felt as if it was coming to an end. Paris in all of its vibrancy couldn't hold me down any more than anywhere else could. Neither could Bruno. I loved him but I knew I had to continue on my journey. There was a force pulling me in a direction and I had to follow. Leaving Bruno behind was one of the hardest things I had ever had to do. It felt so wrong but so necessary at the same time.

I had always dreamed of finding a man I could spend eternity with, a love so strong it could last forever. Was Bruno this man? I don't know. But at the time, I felt the need to continue on exploring the world and exploring other people. It still felt as if my journey was just beginning. Maybe years would pass and I would find myself back in Paris in the arms of Bruno. But right now I had to leave. It was a gut feeling. Bruno had forever changed me and I would hold a piece of him in my heart forever. I knew he felt the same about me.

I know the feeling of love. Love is something real, whether you can see it or not. That *feeling* is eternal. Maybe the physical aspect of love is the part that is fleeting. While Bruno's physical body would not accompany me on my onward journey, the feelings of love I experienced while with him would. Those feelings were somehow a part of who I was.

The experiences we have and the feelings we have are the most real thing there is. Those *feelings* are the only things that are uniquely personal to us. Feelings are more real than your money, your job title, your clothing, or even your physical body.

It is the feeling that can never be taken away.

TWENTY-ONE

TIME AT SEA

———

When I left Paris, I explored a bit more of my surroundings with the money I had saved. I traveled throughout more of France, Switzerland, Germany, Belgium and the Netherlands. While there were quite a few interesting people I met on my European journey, it seemed like no coincidence that I met up with my old friend Samuel one last time. It was winter of 1892 and I found myself in Berlin. It was cold but the city had an icy charm to it. I was bundled up trying to keep warm as I walked down the street. I thought it strange when I heard someone calling out "Annala!" from a distance behind me. It took a couple of yells before I turned around to find Samuel dashing towards me. I should have known we would meet again. I don't know who was more surprised at our chance meeting, him or me. We decided to grab a bite to eat to catch up. He told me about his family, his success with his novel "The Adventures of Huckleberry Finn," his financial troubles, and his daughter

Susie's health problems. So many emotions overtook me as I listened to all of Samuel's stories. He had endured quite a few hardships but I sensed a sarcastic optimism about him, despite all he had gone through. He had spent a good bit of time in various locations around the world, which had opened his eyes to so much more. His experiences had made him more knowledgeable and perceptive. Some of the wisest words he ever said to me were "travel is fatal to prejudice, bigotry, and narrow-mindedness." He had traveled quite a bit and crossed paths with so many different people. I had experienced first hand that people are people. "People are people throughout time and place. No matter where you go, and when, you will find a variety of people that all resemble each other mentally and emotionally." When I said this to Samuel, he smiled and told me he agreed. He also expressed that kindness was of utmost importance. "Kindness is a language which the deaf can hear, and the blind can read," he said to me. I got goose bumps as I listened to these wise words, feeling them to be as true as words can be. I told Samuel about my time spent in Paris and I told him all about Bruno. I found myself missing Bruno greatly upon speaking about him. Samuel had a strange twinkle in his eye as he listened to me speak. I had forgotten about the fact that I still looked youthful. Samuel didn't question why I hadn't aged. I think he knew I wasn't quite human. Maybe he always knew. He had been interested in parapsychology for a while now. Maybe he attributed my presence to something paranormal. Before I left Samuel that day, he gave me a copy of "The Adventures of Huckleberry Finn," a novel that would become one of my all-time favorites. And no, I don't just love it because Samuel was a good friend. I love it because it is truly a masterpiece. That chilly day in Berlin would be the last time I would see Samuel on this earth. Maybe we will cross paths again one day.

As I continued to travel throughout Western Europe, I had a mix of emotions. My heart was torn between traveling east, continuing by land, or returning to the sea. My mind wandered in all different directions. There were days I felt lonely and wanted to return to Bruno and there were days I trusted in my path, wherever it would lead me. I didn't know where to go or what to do. I didn't know if it mattered. I tried to listen to my heart but still found myself lost and confused. I spent a lot of time traveling throughout Germany and decided to slowly head west, spending time in Belgium and then the Netherlands. It was early 1900's when I found myself craving the freedom of the sea. It was time for me to be a mermaid again. It had felt like ages since I had lived in the ocean. The world was changing. So much had happened, not just in the world, but in my personal life as well. The sea would be good for me. I would be able to get away from everything to clear my head.

Like I have mentioned before, while I travel through the sea, time seems to be irrelevant. I often find myself in a dreamlike state thinking about moments and experiences. As I make my way through the water, I am able to rid myself of the notion of time. It is a peculiar and phenomenal feeling to be shooting through space without knowing what "year" it is or what "day" it is. It just is. Everything just is.

In terms of how people view time, decades had passed before I reached land again. In the time I spent at sea, humans had changed the world in ways I never could have imagined. In the 30 years I spent at sea, radio, airplanes, automobiles, and television were invented. The world was a new place for the people living in it. However, inventions weren't the only thing that occurred in my years at sea. One of the deadliest conflicts in human history occurred. World War I left over 17 million people dead and 20 million wounded. Ironically, more people died in the 1918-1919 influenza pandemic than died in World War I.

There was a lot of suffering that occurred while I swam peacefully through the sea. There were brutal battles, painful deaths, and tortured minds. However, there was surely a lot of happiness too. I find it strange to think about all that happened in those 30 years at sea. I was living in my own bubble, calm and free. I didn't know about all the crazy turmoil happening between the humans. I also didn't know about any of the great inventions humans had worked so hard to create. I was in my own world, on my own path. As I delved deeper into this thought, I began to think about how humans live their lives, not much differently than I had been living. Surely, there were people living on land during World War I who were not affected by the battle at all.

There had to have been people who didn't even know a war was happening. I guess what I am trying to say is that it is easy to be unaware or disconnected from something that is happening outside your scope of the world. As you read these words right now, there is someone dying at the hands of another, there is someone suffering from a terrible disease, and there is someone working towards an invention that will change the world. There is so much happening every single day and most people are caught up in their own web of events, they fail to notice the changes. There are times I have had feelings of guilt looking back at all the time I spent away at sea. I was living a peaceful existence, while so many others lived lives of misery. Maybe I should have been on land helping out in some way. Maybe I should have devoted that time to fighting against one of the many injustices that were taking place. However, maybe I needed the time alone, away from the chaos. Sometimes taking a step away from such an ominous force is best. It is not always easy finding a balance between devoting your time to fighting for something versus stepping back and trying to enjoy the natural beauty around us. I guess there is a time for everything. There is a time to fight, a time for peace, a time to speak, a time to listen, a time to believe, and a time to question. Everyone's time is different. It is important to connect to your own personal journey and listen to what you think you should be doing at any moment in time. It may be different from what someone else is doing and that is okay. It might be your time to fight and someone else's time for peace. It's your time.

TWENTY-TWO

ELEPHANTS, SALT, SATYAGRAHA & FLIGHT

—————

India
1930- 1937

A fter my time at sea, I found myself craving adventure once again. I was ready to leave the water for the feeling of earth below my feet. Lured in by the smell of spicy red chili, earthy cumin, savory cardamom, precious cinnamon, and nectarous coconuts dancing through the air, I washed ashore in a magical place. There is something special about India I can't quite explain. Every time I think about India, overwhelming emotions come over me. The land is mysterious and seductive.

From the Arabian Sea, I entered the southwestern part of India now known as Karnataka. As I ventured through the lush forests, I found myself mesmerized by all the plants and animals I came across. Regal tigers stared at me from behind bushes, spotted deer pranced by, and bonnet macaques playfully bounced through the trees curiously following me through the forest. This land put a spell on me. I eventually came across a small hut, deep in the forest. I hadn't encountered any humans yet and I wondered what the people of this land would be like.

As I approached the unkempt hut, I wondered if anyone even lived in it. I slowly crept around it, admiring the beauty of the overgrown shrubs and untrimmed flowers surrounding this home. As I neared the entrance of the house, I saw a man approaching, coming home for the night. He looked surprised to see me. It didn't seem like many people lived in this area.

Garud was a middle-aged Indian man, genuine and content with his simple life in the lovely forest. Though he was in his late 50's he looked much younger. He was healthy, strong and full of life. From the moment I met Garud, I trusted him, sensing his kindness and high sense of morality. Garud didn't know who I was or why I was wandering through this remote land on my own, but he welcomed me into his humble abode. I was happy to have a place to stay and I could tell Garud was excited to have some company as well.

The first evening at Garud's home, I got to know him quite well. He spoke to me about his sons who were working in the city and about the time he spent living and traveling throughout different parts of India. He was very interested in my stories as well, curious to hear about many of my different travel experiences. Garud was extremely knowledgeable. I was surprised that this man who was living in a hut, away from society, knew so much about the world. As I got to know Garud, he became a friend and a guardian in a sense. I found myself content spending time in the jungle, learning so much from Garud. I decided to stay awhile.

Garud had many interests. Above all else, he loved being out in nature. His house was situated near a river. Every day he would go down to the river to watch the elephants bathe. I would follow him through the trees to the river every morning, all the while listening to him as he pointed out the great hornbills, parakeets, kites, eagles, herons, and other various birds that danced through the air. Down by the river, elephants played and rested in peace. As I spent more time with these huge, gentle creatures, I couldn't help but feel a deep connection to them. In a sense, these giant land animals reminded me of the graceful whales that swam through the sea.

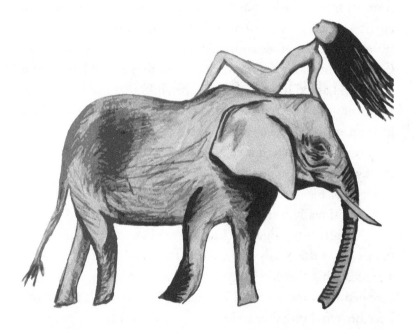

Garud taught me about elephant behavior and told me about all the various elephants he observed on a daily basis. He became close to the elephants and adored each of their different personalities. The serene creatures trusted him and showed him affection. "Elephants are very similar to humans," Garud told me. "They have no problem showing happiness when amongst loved ones, but they have no problem displaying grief as well." I noticed Garud get emotional as he continued. "Much like humans, there is undoubtedly an exceptional bond between a mother and her calf. A mother must constantly be touching her child, walking as her tiny baby walks under her. I have watched mothers bathe their precious babies, haul their babies out of pits and I have watched mothers rush over to a squealing baby in distress." I watched a tear drop from Garud's eye as he went on. "There is nothing sadder in this world than watching an elephant grieve. Not too long ago I witnessed a baby elephant become separated from its mother. The baby would be taken and trained to be a circus animal. As men forcefully tore the two apart, the wails from both the mother and child were unbearable to listen to." Garud pointed out the mother elephant to me. She had a child with her. I asked if that was the same child that had been taken from her. "No," Garud said as he pointed to the young elephant in front of us. "That elephant was only a young boy when his baby sister was taken captive. When it first happened, that young male would wake up in the middle of the night screaming at the thought of his sister being taken away. The mother had spent days emotionally torn apart at what these men did to her. The entire family was damaged. I don't even like to think about the baby now in the hands of the circus handlers. She mustn't have any idea what this life is about. For her, it must be hell." Tears dropped from my eyes as I listened to Garud. I felt angry and heartbroken. Humans can be so selfish and cruel.

I would continue to observe the elephants every day, growing closer and closer to them. I became good friends with certain ones. They trusted me and expressed joy at seeing me when I would meet them down by the river. I found myself constantly asking Garud questions. Garud inspired me with his outlook on life. While he hadn't traveled outside of India, he had an understanding about the world. I never saw Garud anger unless he was speaking about the animals he loved so much. He hated the way many people seemed to have no regard for *all* living things. Garud told me about the importance of all forms of life. He would free the spiders that made their way into his room and the lizards that found themselves trapped between the walls of his home.

Garud also had a deep appreciation for beauty. From the meals he prepared to the way he kept his home tidy and simply decorated, I could sense his artistic nature. I really admired Garud. This simple man taught me so much.

When it came time for me to leave Garud, I felt extremely solemn. I didn't want to leave him alone. However, I knew in my heart he would be just fine. I would be leaving him just as I found him, at peace with himself and the surrounding nature. He had the birds, the whispering winds and the loving elephants to keep him company. He was a happy man. There is never reason to worry about a content person. That person will always be content. Garud told me to be careful on my continued journey. He warned me about the corrupt and wicked side of India I had yet to encounter. I promised him I would be cautious and I bid him farewell.

I headed north along the coast, stopping to cleanse myself in the sea every so often. The salty water always felt so nourishing to me. Salt, simple and pure, is essential to life. Since the beginning of human history, salt has been used as a form of currency, cities have been named based off of salt, and wars have been fought over salt. It seemed ironic that this seemingly abundant substance was such a big deal. However, I thought more about it and it seemed even more ironic that something as useless as paper money, in it's basic form, was an even bigger deal. Combine salt and money and you get what started satyagraha.

It was April of 1930 and I had made my way up to the city of Dandi. I entered the city from the Arabian Sea where I had spent some time soaking my body in the salty waters. Upon arriving in the city, I realized right away that something was happening. I stumbled upon tens of thousands of people marching together. Confused, I asked a local merchant what was going on. He told me the people were protesting the British salt monopoly.

In India at this time, Britain's Salt Acts prohibited Indians from collecting and selling salt. The Indian citizens were forced to purchase the essential mineral from the British who not only had a monopoly over the sale and manufacture of salt but they also applied an excessive salt tax. A man named Mohandas Gandhi decided to lead his people on a march from his ashram at Sabermanti to the coastal town of Dandi (a 240 mile trip) to challenge British policy. He would make salt out of seawater in Dandi, thus defying British rule. Apparently, only 78 people started the march with Gandhi. However, by the time I saw them at Dandi, there were tens of thousands! Millions of Indians in coastal cities all followed in Gandhi's footsteps by making salt and spurring civil disobedience all across India.

Gandhi termed his nonviolent civil disobedience satyagraha. Satyagraha was not just passive resistance. Rather, it signified strength and force through nonviolence. Satya means "truth" in Sanskrit and agraha means "insistence on." Mahatma Gandhi would become famous for leading India into independence. His beliefs, principles and practices gained him recognition all over the world. To this day, Gandhi represents freedom and peace.

It was amazing to see so many people come together to "fight" against a wrong. Watching the sea of people at Dandi was inspiring. It would take years and years before the Indians gained their independence, but this was a start. Truth and justice always prevail. It may take years, decades or even centuries, but in the end, good wins. The Indian citizens were fighting for their freedom. Freedom is always worth fighting for. As a girl of the sea and the world, I can't imagine a life of constraint. This earth is all of ours. One group should never be allowed to control and suppress another group. Nature is the only authority that can ultimately control us.

When I left Dandi, I headed east across the country. On my journey I met all kinds of people. I ate curries and drank teas. I ventured through tiny villages and finally settled in the city of Calcutta. The mysterious and enticing city of Calcutta stirred up all kinds of emotions inside of me.

Horse buggies and cars shared the streets, grand buildings adorned the banks of the Hooghly River, peasants played music outside bazaars, and workers congregated around the city. Calcutta was a cultural center filled with Hindus and Muslims, wealthy landowners and peasants in slums, and British and Indians all living amongst each other. As with any city, there was so much to be amazed by. There were beautiful hotels and gardens, markets with delicious food, and passionate people playing music on the street. However, there were also dilapidated buildings, foul-smelling slums, broken animals pulling people in carriages, and con men lurking amongst the crowds. Beside the beauty, there was a disturbing darkness. My heart stopped every time I passed a dying human on the street or an abused animal tortured at the hands of a human. I would see young mothers with babies begging for food and money on the side of the road. There were old men so skinny and malnourished it looked as if their bodies could snap in half. Every time I passed such an unfortunate individual I would become overwhelmed with hopelessness. I remember seeing a zebra pulling a carriage through the center of the city and feeling sorrowful for this animal that was denied his right to freedom. I saw so much suffering, making me question our existences. What is it that we are all doing on this earth? Why are some beings (human and nonhuman) subject to lifetimes of hardship?

It was in Calcutta that I met Noel. Noel was a British journalist living in Calcutta, writing about East India Company's textile trade. Noel was opinionated, loud and loaded. He came from a well-to-do family in Britain. Noel mingled with the wealthiest as well as with those who had next to nothing. Noel was writing with the intent to shed light on the control Britain was exercising over the textile industry by sending raw materials back to Britain and then re-exporting finished goods to the colonies to be sold at preposterous prices.

I became good friends with Noel. He had a desire to do something meaningful with his life and work toward changing the world, but he also loved partying and luxurious living. Noel was an interesting person. He was very intelligent and had a good sense of humor. He was eloquent and sophisticated. As we became closer, he always wanted me around. He treated me to the finest indulgences, but he never hit on me. I loved his company and I was happy with our friendship. I wouldn't have wanted more than a friendship with him. But I found it peculiar he should want to spend so much time with me without wanting something more. My past experiences with men had showed me that most men would only spend so much time and money on a woman, unless they were hoping for some sort of sexual relationship. Noel would soon open up to me after a night of drinking by confessing for the first time that he was gay. I could tell he was nervous to tell me, never having told anyone before. I was touched he trusted me with his secret and I promised I wouldn't tell anyone. Noel feared his parents would be disappointed should he open up to them. I have never understood why anyone would care about such a thing, but I have found many people are closed-minded until society evolves as a whole. After opening up to me, Noel and I became even closer, feeling free to speak our minds to one another.

Time went by and Noel became my best friend. Many of his friends assumed we were a couple and I always played along. As long as Noel was uncomfortable being open about his sexuality, I would hold on to his secret. Eventually, Noel asked me if I wanted to go to London with him to meet his family. He told me he wanted to finally tell them he was gay, and he wanted me by his side when he did so. I wasn't so sure about making a trip all the way to England for that sole purpose, but Noel was insistent. I finally agreed to accompany him. Noel's riches bought us a trip few people were able to experience back then. For the first time in both my and Noel's life, we traveled by air. The experience was unreal. Boarding the metal Imperial Airways plane is something I will never forget. It marked a turning point. In a week, one could be on the other side of the world by traveling on a flying boat! There were only 15 other passengers on our plane and we traveled in style. I spent the majority of my days in the sky looking out the window, in awe at the fast-changing world. I slept a bit when I could and tried to stay warm on the chilly plane. Many people felt nauseous and used the bowls by their beds when they got sick. We must have made at least 10 stops over the course of our days, but we finally made it to England!

I would be staying with Noel until I figured out my next move. Noel took me all over London, which was a modern city of wonder. Electric lighting and motor vehicles replaced gas lighting and horse drawn carriages in this efficient city. Noel also introduced me to his family who were all overjoyed to meet me. They were so happy Noel had finally brought a woman home, one they hoped he intended on marrying. We had a big dinner planned with Noel's parents. Tonight was the night Noel planned on revealing his secret. I could tell Noel was nervous, but I assured him his parents would love him no matter what.

As we sat around the dinner table, eating all kinds of delicacies, Noel expressed that he had something to share. His mother looked at me and smiled. I smiled back awkwardly, awaiting Noel's next words. Noel glanced at me and back at his parents. Finally, he blurted out "we're getting married!" His mom jumped up yelling with joy, while I must have looked lost and confused. His parents got up and hugged the two of us and I forced a smile on my face.

When dinner was over, Noel and I headed back to his apartment in the center of the city. I didn't say anything to him. I didn't know what to say. Honestly, I was mad at him. He brought me into something that should have never involved me. I didn't want to marry him. What would his parents think of me when I didn't marry him?

Noel finally broke the silence between us with the famous words, "I'm sorry." I just looked at him. He continued, "I couldn't tell them. Did you see how happy my mom was? She would have been devastated had I told her the truth." As Noel continued to justify his latest mistake, I felt bad for him. I couldn't stay angry with him. He was dealing with an internal battle I knew nothing about.

We got back to Noel's apartment and sat on the couch. He started to cry and told me he didn't know what to do. I felt so sorry for him. I had seen people physically suffering from malnutrition and backbreaking labor in India, but this mental distress seemed to be just as bad in a sense. Noel had more money than anyone I knew, but he suffered just the same. Suffering, much like love or jealousy or fear, is a feeling so personal to an individual, one can only try to imagine what another person is actually feeling. I stayed with Noel and hugged him through the night.

Noel decided he wanted to fly once again. He told me England would soon be at war with Germany and he wanted to go far far away. I thought he was running from himself, but I didn't say anything. He said he wanted to go to Australia. I wondered what Australia would be like. I hadn't been to that land since the 1300s! The only Australians I knew were the aborigines I lived with a long time ago. I was sure the land must have changed in so many ways. He asked if I wanted to go with him. I thought about it, but decided against it. I needed to continue on my own journey, as did he.

Noel's trip from London to Brisbane would be 11 days long with 12 stops in between. It was incredible humans had invented a way to get from one place to another through flight! What seemed like a short trip back then, would only become easier in years to come. It's hard to believe that now, in 2015, that same flight would be only 22 hours with just one stop! What will travel be like 100 years from now? I am excited to find out.

While I didn't accompany Noel to Australia, I did take him up on his offer to buy me a plane ticket. I loved being below the sea, but there was something exhilarating about being so high up in the air. I was ready for flight again. I said goodbye to Noel. He hugged me and told me he loved me. I loved him too. I hope he found peace with himself and I am sure he did some great things with his life.

Next stop: South Africa.

TWENTY-THREE

STRANGELY FAMILIAR

South Africa
1937

Johannesburg was an exquisite place filled with the energy of adventurous souls from all over the world. This city of gold lured in brilliant minds and thrill seekers alike.

I got a job doing clerical work for a big gold mining company. It was there that I met Anje. She came from an Afrikaner farming family who had been struggling in recent years, pushing her to look for work in the city. Anje was strangely familiar. Upon meeting her, I felt as if I knew her. She reminded me so much of a girl named Ciosa I knew back in Italy during the Renaissance. It is not that they looked so much alike, but more so that they acted so much alike.

Anje was adaptable, hard working, intelligent, open-minded and kind. Though she was raised on a farm, she quickly learned the ways of city life, becoming one of the most respected workers in the office. Anje and I clicked right off the bat. We formed an immediate friendship, trusting and opening up to one another. I have realized throughout my years that there are certain beings you automatically connect with. It is almost as if you are on the same frequency, forming a common understanding between the two of you. These special connections we make are the ones that are not easily broken. I have crossed paths with many along my journey, most of which I only formed loose ties with. Those loose ties don't really mean much. Yet, there are a smaller number of extraordinary beings that almost seem placed in your path for a reason. Those special bonds are the ones that inspire us to grow and be better.

I felt at peace in Anje's company. I could be myself and say how I felt without feeling judged or looked down upon. I'm sure she felt the same way around me. The more time I spent with her, the more she reminded me of Ciosa. Their expressions and actions were almost identical. I had experienced this before with people I had met throughout the years. There is no doubt you are bound to meet people that remind you of others. People are people. It is pretty cool when you meet people from totally different parts of the planet who remind you of one another. It just goes to show everyone is the same deep down. Yet, with Anje and Ciosa, the similarities seemed more than just coincidental.

I started to wonder if it could be possible that this was the same being. Could Ciosa have come back to this earth in the form of Anje? Could it be possible that when beings die, they come back to this earth in another form? Maybe an ant comes back as a lizard or a cat comes back as a human? Could I have once been on this earth in the form of something else? Maybe even a human?

I started coming up with all kinds of ideas and theories. Of course nobody knows what happens when we die, but it can be fun to speculate about. I have found that various religions try to explain death in different ways. It is interesting to hear all the different opinions people have about what happens when we die. Some have more positive outlooks on death and some have more negative outlooks. Personally, I don't think death is something to fear. I have never believed in the ideas of heaven and hell. I especially don't believe that anything dies and goes to a hell worse than the hell that can be experienced here on earth. Some creatures are subject to such lifetimes of suffering that their existence here is in hell. However, this earth is also a heaven for others. I think it is important to follow that conscience we are all born with in order to live a moral and fulfilled life. By doing so, there is no reason to fear whatever happens when we depart. There is no specific religion that will get you to a better place when you die. Living with love is all you can do.

Anje and I would speak about all these ideas. Just like me, she loved speculating about all the possibilities of life. We spoke about the meaning of life and what humans are here to do during their short stays here on Earth. We also spoke about animals and their significance to the planet. We pondered whether all things are created equal. Are some beings more enlightened than others? Are some beings tuned into something others aren't? None of us know much of anything but Anje and I agreed that love is of utmost importance. If we do nothing else with our lives, live with love.

I remember the day I met Makoma. She arrived at our office, looking for a clerical job. I remember her being soft-spoken and a bit timid when she walked in, looking for someone in charge so that she could apply. When speaking to the manager, I heard him tell her we weren't hiring. Two days later, a different girl walked in. She was looking for work as well. However, this time around, the manager asked her to apply. When I realized Makoma wasn't hired because she was black, I felt angry and confused. Why would skin color make any difference as to what kind of worker someone was?

South Africa was an interesting place at this time. There was such a division between groups of people. There were the British whites that owned most of the mines and had most of the money. Then there were the Afrikaners. The Afrikaners (Anje was Afrikaner) were white South Africans typically of Dutch descent. There were the black South Africans who were at the bottom of the totem pole when it came to acquiring jobs and were treated unjustly in many ways solely because of their skin color. Finally, there were immigrants. There were a fairly large number of Jewish immigrants who migrated from Europe due to increased tensions leading up to World War II. However, in the year that I arrived in South Africa, The Aliens Act of 1937 paused Jewish immigration for years.

As I have said before, those with money and power can and will control. The British whites had the money and power in South Africa at this time and there is no doubt they used it to control anyone and everyone they could. That doesn't mean every single white British person was to blame, just certain ones in power.

About a week after Makoma applied for a job in our office, I saw her walking about in the city. As she passed me in the street, I stopped her and told her I recognized her. "You were in my place of work the other day," I told her. She smiled, seemingly recognizing me as well. "I have been looking for work all over the city," she said. "It is not easy for a girl like me." I told her I was on my way to meet my friend Anje for lunch and asked if she would like to join. She accepted.

Because Makoma would not be able to eat in a restaurant reserved for only whites, we went to a kaferaiteh. Mostly blacks came to eat here and it was not the cleanest of restaurants, but it was okay nonetheless. This kaferaiteh was nicer than most, though it was far from nice. The three of us ordered soup and hot tea. I could tell Makoma was grateful I invited her along and she kept thanking me as if I did something so extraordinary for her. The truth was, I didn't understand why humans had created so many rules to separate everyone. Anje and I were on the same page when it came to rules. If a rule didn't make sense to us, we wouldn't be so quick to follow it. While many other "whites" would never be caught spending time with a "black," Anje and I were atypical of society. In fact, I thought the more people see others intermixing, the more accepting they may become.

At the kaferaiteh, we had a server named Miriam. She was very friendly and there was something about her I really liked. Miriam had a positive energy one could immediately sense through her genuine smile. Miriam was a Jewish immigrant from Lithuania. Her family had migrated to South Africa just a couple years ago. Miriam could earn a decent living working at the kaferaiteh, but her hours were long and the work was not highly respected.

Makoma ended up finding work nearby; working for a Jewish immigrant family who sold used clothing. Anje, Makoma, and I decided we would meet for lunch every week. We always visited Miriam at the same kaferaiteh, becoming friends with her. Miriam would sit down with us and chat about whatever we were talking about that day. The four of us were an unlikely group- a white Afrikaner, a black African, a Jewish immigrant, and a mermaid (well, they didn't know that). Many people actually assumed I was British, having picked up a bit of an accent from all my time spent with Noel. We all became good friends and in a sense, I felt as if they became my family for the time. I knew we could all count on one another and despite our different backgrounds, we all understood each other.

I spent the most time with Anje, working with her on a daily basis. Though Anje came from an Afrikaner family, she did not share in all her family's beliefs. Some members of her family believed in the Afrikaner Nationalist movement, many of which believed they were "chosen to rule South Africa." It was complicated because the white Afrikaners often had to compete with the black Africans to acquire jobs. Therefore, many white Afrikaners supported racially discriminatory legislation. Because the white British had most of the control, Afrikaners came together to form their own banks, insurance companies, and other businesses so that they would not be under the control of the British. You see, nothing is ever black and white (not even the blacks and whites). I could understand the Afrikaners wanting to fight for their right to obtain higher paying jobs and resist control. Yet, after awhile, the Afrikaner movement would grow so big, these people that were once trying to free themselves from the suppression of the British, were now creating laws discriminating against blacks, Asians, and Jews. This was the beginning of the ideology of apartheid.

Anje and I spoke about the idea of separation. Her and I agreed it didn't seem fair to separate people based off of color or religion, or anything for that matter. Anje told me "many of my people are scared the black Africans will take their jobs. However, I don't think that is a valid fear. If someone has a skill, whether they are black, white, or anything else, they can use that skill for work. It seems unfair to say someone shouldn't be able to work in a certain position because they are black. If they are good at the job, why not?" I agreed with Anje. Fear often turns people to control others, but one should never act out of fear.

I had seen groups control and suppress one another countless times throughout time and place. However, I had also seen first hand that people were becoming more open and tolerant toward one another. Though there was still a lot of hate and discrimination, there were a lot of open minded and accepting people. I think the ease of travel was uniting the world like never before. This is a bold statement to make about a time leading up to World War II, but I stand by that statement.

I loved having a friend like Anje. She was the type of person you could talk about anything with. She never angered and she always offered a rational opinion. I wondered if she was meant to be in my life to teach me something. Could I be in her life to teach her something as well? It certainly seemed as if we learned a lot from one another, whether we realized it in the moment or not. Maybe Anje was Ciosa, here to remind me that fear shouldn't influence your decisions, ideas I once discussed with Ciosa during the Renaissance. In a society filled with so many people who seemingly followed along with the rules society placed before them, maybe we were here to remind each other that rules are often arbitrary. Maybe we were here to "break the rules." Just by spending time with Makoma we were breaking the rules in a sense. We weren't following the guidelines this society set for girls like us and that is sometimes enough to make a statement.

TWENTY-FOUR

TRAPPED

———

Lithuania
1939-1945

L eaving South Africa was bittersweet for me. I had grown to really love the vibrant city of Johannesburg and the serenity of the surrounding wild lands. Saying goodbye to Anje was difficult, but maybe she would enter my life again one day, maybe in another form. I hoped to return to this lovely land someday, but now it was time for me to move forward.

It was 1939 and I found myself in the vast land of Russia. It was a strange time in my life. As I traveled through Russia, the frigid climate and gloomy skies contributed to the built-up tension that was caused by World War II. Life felt rigid and systematic in this land during the war. People were living day by day and there was a sense of hopelessness in the air.

I traveled across Russia before crossing into Latvia and then Lithuania. It was 1940 when I decided to settle in Vilnius, the capital of Lithuania. Lithuania, occupied by the Soviet Union, was undergoing many changes. Where I lived, a Soviet government was set up so that Vilnius became the new capital of the Lithuanian SSR.

In the years prior to my arrival, Vilnius had gone through many transitions. It would be hard to imagine the vast changes that would take place in the years to come. It was June of 1941 when the Germans captured Vilnius. Every single day, more and more changes started to occur. The changes did not seem to be happening for the better. Ghettos were set up in the old town for the Jewish people, thus separating them further. I thought about Miriam, my South African friend who had moved from Lithuania less than 10 years ago. What would life be like for her now had she stayed?

It is hard to write about the period of time that I spent in Lithuania. There was a haunting chill in the air. People were fearful. But people were still living day by day, just taking everything as it came. The best way for me to describe the feeling I got from my experiences in Vilnius is the feeling of being trapped. As a mermaid, I have always found refuge in the sea. I have always been able to hop in the ocean and go wherever I wanted to go. However, as I observed the people living around me, I felt a deep sadness as I realized most people could not escape their situations so easily. Between 1941 and 1944 tens of thousands of people were executed near the railway station of Ponary, not too far from where I had been living. The Nazis would round up Jews from the ghettos and kill them in mass numbers. The construction of an oil storage facility had been started near Ponary before Nazi Germany occupied the area. However, because the project was left unfinished, the Nazis decided to use the large oil storage pits as a place to dispose of bodies. Only 7,000 of the 70,000 Jews living in Vilnius survived the war.

The war brought out the best and worst in people. It was a strange time. Looking back, the holocaust almost seems like a dark nightmare. It is hard to believe that millions of people were systematically murdered. The amount of suffering that occurred at this time was unimaginable. The people that were sent off to concentration camps, separated from their families and murdered were trapped in a time and place they were unable to escape. So many people's existences consisted of darkness, complete darkness. I am sure many people questioned why the world was so cruel. I found myself asking the same question. During this hopeless time, many people experienced what can only be described as hell. Death was likely a relief, which saddens me beyond words. I wondered why I was so lucky. So many people live tortured lives, trapped in the circumstances of their place and time. Yet, here I was, living an existence longer than most and able to see the world from so many different angles. My perspectives on the world are so much broader than most ever experience. I have a broad worldview, whereas most people form opinions based on their very short stays in one location here on earth, thus making it more difficult to understand the happenings beyond their scope.

As I thought about the feeling of being entrapped, freedom became ever more important to me. No being should ever be subject to an existence of slavery and torture at the hands of another. Humans are not the only beings entitled to freedom. All living creatures should be entitled to their freedom. This earth is all of ours and I truly believe we all serve a purpose. Rather than focusing on suppressing one another, I think we need to focus on working together and figuring out what each of us has to offer.

I experienced the darkness that accompanied the Second World War firsthand. It was an ominous time that left me questioning the purpose of the bizarre lives we all live. We all have such personal journeys and I wondered why so many people had to undergo lives of suffering. Whatever surrounds you becomes your reality. My reality is constantly changing as I go from place to place over time. During World War II, I questioned the reality I was surrounded by. This solemn time was the only reality many knew. When I finally left Lithuania in 1945, I headed straight for the Baltic Sea. I became extremely emotional upon entering the water. I was free and alive. Why? Who was I and what was I doing here? My heart told me to keep going. Something told me that I needed to continue on my journey, adventuring and learning. Though I had recently experienced a cruel, cold world, I knew there was much beauty and happiness to be experienced as well.

I hoped the sea would reawaken me. I hoped the wind would push me toward something new and enlightening. Wherever I was going, I hoped it would be good. In the sea, I was free at last. I had hope once again.

TWENTY-FIVE

NATURE HEALS

In time, nature heals all. This is a lesson I have learned along the way. After leaving Lithuania, I felt worn out and weak. I had spent too much time in my small, cage-like apartment. The recent skies had been foggy and haunting. The world was at war and destruction was everywhere. I felt as if machines had taken over. Not only had humans created machines that could destroy the world, but humans themselves were acting as killing machines. Everything seemed bleak, rigid and uncompromising. However, upon entering the sea, and seeing the sun and blue sky, my energy started to shift. The weather was clearing up, my skin was soaking in the water and my eyes were opened to divine beauty once again. The amazing thing about nature is its purity. No man-made object can ever compare to the true radiance of nature.

As I traveled through the sea I started to feel healthy and alive again. I noticed magic happening all around me. I was reunited with the creatures of the sea, proving to me that life consists of so much more than what humans create on land. I saw birth and death, I watched colorful clouds form patterns in the sky, I listened to the creatures communicating as they swam around me, I tasted what I can only describe as the bittersweet taste of earth, and I felt at home and at peace. It was amazing that my energy could shift so suddenly upon my emergence into the natural world.

Whenever I feel lost or depressed, I have found that simply spending time outside, in nature, is the best medicine there is.

The wind brushing against your skin, the sound of birds chirping and leaves rustling, and the smell of the crisp terrene is enough to make anyone feel better.

I have also found that nature is almighty. Though humans have changed the world with unbelievable inventions, nothing is more powerful than nature. It is important to realize this fact. I think we, as creatures of the earth, need to work with nature. Nature provides us with everything we need; it is just a matter of harnessing the powers of nature so that all living things can coexist on this heavenly planet. Nature needs to be our partner, not our enemy.

As I dove deep into the sea, danced alongside dolphins, and surfaced to watch days starting and coming to an end, I gained a newfound excitement. I was alive. Nature had healed my soul, as it had before and as it would again.

TWENTY-SIX

STARTING OVER, AGAIN AND AGAIN

Iceland
~1955

ere I was in a land that was new to me. When I first came
ashore on Iceland, I wondered once again what life had in
store for me this time around. It seemed I was constantly starting over, integrating myself into a culture and people I hadn't
experienced before. While people are people across land and
time, inventions, styles and trends are constantly changing. It
is a strange feeling to enter a new land to find people practicing different ways of life. I never know what to expect. Will I
encounter a group of people who believe women must be covered
from head to toe, or a group of people half-naked? Will there be
cars on the road or planes in the sky? Will there be things I have
never seen before? The future would hold cellular phones and the
Internet, inventions that were unimaginable to me at this point in
my life. I had washed ashore on lands to find that people across

the globe no longer needed to use fire as a source of light or heat. I had come to find that people would use TV as a new form of entertainment. I even remember the first time I saw a printed book, long before so many of the other inventions that would leave me in awe! There were endless possibilities. However, every time I came to a new land, I came to realize that time would have since shifted ways of life and the current world. On the simplest of levels, thoughts on my personal integration in this new world always occupied my mind. What clothing would I need to wear, how should I fix my hair, and what accessories would I need to acquire in order to look "normal" in this particular society? What new technologies would I need to learn? What mode of transportation would I use to get around? Starting over is never easy.

These thoughts occupied my mind as I first stepped foot on the land of Iceland. I traveled the land and admired the natural beauty of the mountains, bays, fjords, geysers and blue lagoons. I watched the Northern Lights and continued to let Earth's charm amaze me with each new day.

It was in Húsavík that I met Sesil. Sesil was a fisherman and the owner of a small restaurant. I met Sesil on a chilly evening in town. I was eating at a local restaurant near the sea when Sesil decided to come over and start a conversation with me. I had just arrived in Húsavík and I think Sesil could tell I was from out of town. As we started talking, I quickly realized Sesil was the owner of the restaurant. When Sesil found out I was looking for work, he offered me a job without hesitation. He told me he could use my help around the small restaurant, both helping serve people as well as with some of the business work. I was happy to help and I needed the money.

Upon meeting Sesil, I immediately liked him. He was an older man with a wisdom that can't be taught. I think Sesil was drawn to me because though I was seemingly young, I had experienced many things. It didn't take long for me to consider Sesil a friend. We could talk for hours and his thoughts always sparked ideas of my own.

Sesil had gone through a lot in his lifetime. He had lost his wife and one son many years ago. He had lived in many different places and had many different jobs. I know life had been rough for him at times, but he still kept a spark about him. I particularly remember a conversation Sesil and I had one foggy morning over a cup of coffee in the restaurant. Sesil and I were talking about the inevitability of change. "One should never fear change," Sesil said. "Nothing stays the same. Those who try to hold onto something that is bound to change will never fully be happy. The key is being able to let go and adapt. It is not the smartest, strongest or richest that survives. It is the most adaptable that survives." As I listened to Sesil, I got to thinking. He was right. I had witnessed his words to be true throughout all the time I had spent traveling the earth. It seemed that the species that could adapt to this ever-changing world were the ones to persevere.

In Iceland, the land of fire and ice, change was inevitable. The continent's sizzling volcanic springs caress some of Europe's biggest glaciers. It seemed Iceland was an appropriate place to talk about change. The land of Iceland itself is constantly undergoing geographic construction as volcanoes regularly erupt and ice melts and carves the land. The powerful forces of nature have contributed almighty waterfalls, bubbling hot springs, steep-sided fjords and valleys, and exuberant green meadows to the fast-changing island. This rugged land teeming with unique animals, magnificent lava flows and booming waterfalls makes for an exquisitely beautiful place. Speaking to Sesil about change stirred my mind. I was ready to explore a bit more of Iceland before moving on. It would be hard to leave Húsavík, but this wouldn't be the first (or last) time I would be heading onward.

Letting go is not always easy, but trusting that everything will work out for the best is the only way to live. I looked deeper into the life I was living and realized adaptability was crucial for me. Constantly having to start over every time I happened upon a new land made me learn to embrace change. The wonderful experiences we have are fleeting, but worth it nonetheless. I know that life will always have its ups and downs, but as you learn to love the "new," life seems to place endless opportunities in your path. The talk of change got me excited. I hadn't been in Iceland long but I was enticed by thoughts of new experiences. I had heard about the low-cost trans-Atlantic flights offered by Loftleiðir Icelandic. As many young Americans would later use this airline as a cheap way to get to Europe, Loftleiðir Icelandic (Icelandic Airlines) would soon earn the nickname "Hippie Airline." I was excited to fly across the Atlantic for the first time! I was heading to America to start over, again.

TWENTY-SEVEN

EXPIRATION DATE

America
1960-1965

W hen I arrived in America in 1960, I felt change in the air. New ideas were being discussed and people were fighting for equality, environmental protection and freedom. I felt alive and excited to be in the fast-changing country of America where new concepts and beliefs spread through the air like pollen being carried by the wind.

I took my time venturing across the United States, stopping in different cities and taking different jobs along the way. As always, I met all kinds of people. Most people were nice, many were helpful, but certain select individuals were inspiring beyond words.

It was 1963 when I found myself in the state of California. It was here that I became good friends with a man named Ken. Ken was an interesting person. He had so many ideas and dreams, something I really admired about him. He also had many experiences he shared with me that made me, an already curious person, even more inquisitive. Ken told me about his experience working as a night aide at the Menlo Park Veterans Hospital. It was there that he volunteered to take part in Project MKULTRA (this turned out to be a study financed by the CIA). Under the project, which studied the effects of psychoactive drugs on people, Ken had experiences with LSD, cocaine, psilocybin, and mescaline. As Ken told me about his experiences with some of these drugs, I couldn't help but relate it to my experience with mushrooms in the Amazon, a long time ago. I told Ken about my trip with Ti and he was enthralled by my accounts of what happened in the Amazon. He told me I had to try LSD, a drug that was legal at the time and a drug he came to be particularly fond of. I am very much a yes person, especially when I trust and respect the person influencing me to try something new, so I told him I was interested. What I really admired about Ken was not only his drive and creativity, but also his compassion. Ken told me about his experiences in the Veterans hospital and how he was inspired to write "One Flew Over the Cuckoo's Nest." He expressed his idea that the patients he dealt with in the hospital were not insane like society made them out to be. Rather he believed these people were pushed out because they did not act the way society expected them to act. I thought about this idea more as I thought about my travels through place and time. I had certainly found that different cultures expressed different ideas for what was "normal." However, everyone is different and not everyone fits into the standards of "normal" that society places before them. Experiences also influence the actions of an individual, and everyone experiences different things. I have said before that I am quite adaptable, thus, making it easy for me to seemingly blend in whatever society I happen to be in. However, I find that I am usually drawn to the outcasts of society. I am drawn to the people who don't fit in with whatever "normal" is and the people who question the standards of society. I think this is why Ken and I got along so well.

I grew extremely close to Ken and his wife Faye as well as many of their other acquaintances. It was June of 1964 when I decided to join Ken and a group of our other friends on a cross-country journey from La Honda, California to New York. Ken bought an old, decked out school bus, which had a kitchen, a bathroom and bunks, and added a sound system, a generator, and a railed in seating platform on top of the bus. We helped Ken paint the bus with all different colors and designs. It was the most artistic vehicle I had ever seen! I was excited to take this journey across America with my fellow Pranksters, as Ken called us.

I knew the entire trip would probably take about a month. Some people would join in different locations, and others would be left behind. Ken brought enough LSD, speed and marijuana to go around. This next month would be a party to say the least.

Though I knew the next month would be a blast, I was happy it would only be for a certain amount of time. Knowing there was an end date made it that much more special. In a sense, it was a relief knowing I would be able to come back to California in a month and go back to living my *own* life. As I thought about the idea of having an expiration date, I realized that experiences are often more enjoyable when they are not forever. The same holds true for jobs, relationships and life in general. I had many jobs that I knew I would only be working at for say, a year. Because I knew from the beginning there was an expiration date, I took as much out of the experience as I could. I learned as much as I could, I worked as hard as I could, and I loved those around me with all of my heart. Knowing that I would not be working that particular job forever made me appreciate the job that much more. I took what I could from the experience and moved on. It also made the situation less hopeless. For me, the idea of forever takes away from the excitement and energy that comes with a time sensitive situation. The same held true for relationships. I had dated guys that I knew I would not be with forever. I had also made great friends that I knew would not be in my life forever. Having a limited time with someone forces you to connect deeper and love harder. I started thinking about humans and the short amount of time they had on this earth. I wished I could tell them how precious their short stays here are. There is so much to love and enjoy. Many people waste so much time worrying about minor issues and I think they often forget their time here is limited. Knowing there is an end makes everything that much more extraordinary.

The trip up to New York was a colorful blend of events. Our bus, named Further, drew quite a bit of attention! Everyone on board was out to have a good time. We were all on this journey together, open to experience anything life threw our way, enjoying every moment of it. The plan was to film our adventure and create a movie afterwards. This helped when the police stopped us. When they questioned what we were doing, we merely stated we were filmmakers and were let off the hook. So much happened on the forward venture. We spent a couple days at our friend's house in California and painted his swimming pool, we got stuck in the sand in Arizona and decided to trip on LSD while waiting for a tractor to relieve us, and our friend Neil took us out to party on the town in New Orleans. I remember drunkenly suggesting we go night swimming in Lake Ponchartrain and we ended up swimming in the "blacks only area." To me, the lake was for everyone. Why divide it into sections for blacks, whites or anything else? I have so many memories from the trip up to New York that will stay with me forever.

When we arrived in New York at the end of June, we met up with some more people, partied on, and visited the World's Fair. I was enthralled by the World Fair, which was dedicated to "Man's Achievement on a Shrinking Globe in an Expanding Universe" with a theme of "Peace Through Understanding." I had already begun to believe the earth was becoming much more united and connected through ease of travel. It seemed that people had begun to feel the same way. This fair included an exciting blend of culture and technology. It was at this fair that I had my first interaction with computer equipment, decades before individuals around the world would conveniently have their own computers and be able to use the Internet. The world was changing fast. It seemed to be changing quicker and quicker, new technologies being invented at an exponential rate. It was an exciting and hopeful time for the future.

However, not everything I saw gave me hope and excitement. I remember attending a circus event for the first time in New York. As I watched tigers, bears, sea lions, and elephants forced to perform, I felt a deep sadness for these wild animals. I remembered Garud's stories about the elephants taken captive in India and I questioned the so-called progress humans were making. How could it be that there were so many great changes occurring, yet there was still so much unnecessary suffering as well? When would humans realize that all living things have the same emotions and feel pain just the same? I hoped in time the world would wake up to these cruelties. Slowly, it would. Just as there were movements to fight for the rights of blacks, gays and women, there would also be movements to fight for the rights of animals. We are all here together. No living creature, human or non-human, should be enslaved, tortured or oppressed.

At the same time, there was a lot of talk about the Vietnam War. Americans started to see that no country is innocent in war. America was committing the same atrocities that seem to always be committed in war. There was talk of revolution in the air and the youth started to express an air of anti-society. As in any time of tension, the war brought out the best and the worst in people. As hopeless and dark as things seemed for the humans, there was plenty of light as well. I was left with a bittersweet taste in my mouth as I departed from New York City. When we headed home from New York, we journeyed through Canada a bit and ended up back in California in August. What a wild trip it had been. I had seen and experienced so much in just a month. It is amazing how one can have tons of new experiences in a matter of days, or spend countless years doing the same thing everyday. One can do so much (or so little) with their given time.

Ken wanted to edit the footage when we arrived back in California. He decided to throw parties every weekend at his place where people would come and listen to live music, often by the Grateful Dead (Ken's favorite band), and view the progress of the movie edits. I attended a couple of parties, happy to reunite with many of the other Pranksters, but soon enough, I felt the need to continue on my own journey. The wind was summoning me and I had to listen.

The experiences I had with Ken and the rest of the group were life changing. However, like everything else, they came to an end. And it was for the best. My time with the Pranksters expired, but I enjoyed the ride.

TWENTY-EIGHT

THE HIPPIE TRAIL

Luxembourg → Bangkok
1966-1967

Traveling was not something that was new to me, however, the idea of backpacking was becoming ever more popular amongst the young and curious. It was exciting to see how ease of travel was transporting people all over the world like never before. It was 1966 when I hopped on Icelandic Airlines to Luxembourg. Many young Americans, western Europeans, Japanese, and Australians were interested in seeing the world. These young travelers were generally traveling on a budget for extended periods of time. Rather than "vacationing," backpackers were more interested in mingling with locals and experiencing different cultures. Many of the new friends I made while traveling across America spoke about the hippie trail, a route between Europe and South Asia.

I started my backpacking journey in Luxembourg with no real plan along the way. For the first time in my life I stayed in a hostel. The idea of a hostel was magnificent to me. For a small amount of money, anyone could get a bunk in a dorm for the night. Hostels generally had community bathrooms, showers and a kitchen. Rooms could be mixed or single-sex and usually contained anywhere from 4 to 8 beds. My favorite thing about hostels was the fact that so many people from all different backgrounds came together in a single spot. Travelers from different parts of the planet were able to share their thoughts and experiences in their temporary "home" for the night.

I found that because a lot of the travelers I met along the way had a certain curiosity and drive to see the world, it was easy for me to connect with so many of them. It seemed to me that backpackers were inquisitive, seeking knowledge through experience. I was able to relate to the hopeful, big-eyed, gypsy-souled humans who were living day-by-day and city-by-city. These nomadic people bonded in ways one can only understand through experience. Every hostel I stayed at in each new city, I found a new "family" for my short time there. Us backpackers looked out for one another, trusting each other and opening our hearts to one another as if we had known each other for a lifetime. Of course certain individuals made more of an impact on me than others, but there was something special about the backpacking community.

The uncertainty of each and every day made for an even grander adventure. Though I had traveled in a similar manner throughout my life, my experience along the hippie trail was different from my usual migratory lifestyle. On the hippie trail, I was constantly on the move, taking buses from city to city, exploring new locations with new friends, and partying much more often. There were popular spots where backpackers congregated along the trail. I spent months traveling by bus, trains and occasional hitchhiking. It was amazing how easy it had become to get from place to place. It was even more amazing to see how many people were doing it. After backpacking my way through Europe, I spent a good amount of time trekking through Turkey, Israel, Iran, Afghanistan, Pakistan, India and Nepal. I found myself eating flavorful puddings at the famous Pudding Shop in Istanbul, drinking Goldstar beer in Tel Aviv, sipping hot tea in Tabriz, napping in the colorful gardens of Karachi, eating sweet pomegranates in Multan, meandering through street markets in Ludhiana and strolling through Freak Street in Kathmandu. I then started my journey through Southeast Asia. As I hiked my way through Myanmar, Laos, and Thailand, I couldn't help but feel a cosmic charm in the air. I felt as if I was exactly where I needed to be, experiencing what I needed to experience. I also found myself steering away from the typical "backpacker trail." Though I loved the time I spent sticking to the hippie route, I had also experienced the hypocrisies that accompany any sort of group activity. I met some truly inspirational people on my backpacking journey, but by the time I reached Southeast Asia, I found myself craving much needed time on my own. It had been easy to get caught up in the constant partying that seemed to accompany traveling with young, impassioned travelers. Though I love partying, I have found that I need time to cleanse my body and my mind as well, something that can't be done while partying every day. There needs to be a balance.

By the time I reached Myanmar, I freed myself from the system and made my way back into nature. I traveled deep into jungles, bathed under crystal falls and made my way to Laos and then Thailand. As always, travel opened my eyes to the good and bad sides of humanity. Side by side I saw exploitation and I saw beauty. I thought a lot about the war in Vietnam. At this point in my travels I was very close to where so much strife was occurring. I wondered what kinds of anguish people were enduring at this time. I got emotional as I thought about suffering. I thought about mass suffering but I also thought about individual suffering. It was hard to wrap my head around the amount of suffering that occurs every single day. Why? Was any of it necessary?

I spent a good amount of time traveling through Thailand. Though my mind was often occupied with thoughts of suffering, I saw so much beauty and so much happiness during my journey. I found grace in nature as I watched colorful birds chirping charmingly around me, I felt pure happiness as I watched children playfully running and laughing together by the river, and I felt hopeful as I watched so many beings living harmoniously together. There was so much good. More good than bad, I was sure. My final stop in Thailand was Bangkok. This wild city left me with so many mixed emotions. I walked through busy streets lined with vendors selling everything from snake blood to fried scorpions, I floated along the Chao Phraya by boat, drank copious amounts of Mekhong at local bars, and I saw enough to understand why Bangkok acquired the nickname "Sin City of Asia." I did my final bit of partying in the alluringly wicked city of Bangkok before heading south to the sea. I had been backpacking for a good 8 months now and delving into the sea felt necessary. I felt light, free and at peace in the clear waters off of Thailand. I ventured by way of the ocean stopping for short amounts of time in Malaysia, Singapore and Indonesia. This earth has so many unbelievable places. Even after centuries of travel, it continues to blow my mind.

I experienced so much during my backpacking adventure, but what excited me most was the fact that the ease of travel was uniting the world like never before. Anyone with a desire to see the world, no longer needed to spend a ton of money or time making his or her way to the other side of the earth. People had reasonable options as far as places to stay, and travel by bus, train, and even planes had become less expensive over time. In addition, the locals in the poorer countries were exposed to the travelers and these more frequent interactions between people from all walks of life were slowly uniting people like never before. As a girl who values experiences, more than money, security or material objects, it was inspiring to see so many young people choose experiences over anything else. Backpackers were spending their time and money in exchange for experiences rather than the stability of a corporate job, rather than the latest fashionable accessories and rather than the safety of their comfort zone. I was hopeful for the future.

TWENTY-NINE

DEVASTATION AT HOME

I have stated before that in a sense, the ocean is my home. Though I mimic a human on land, while at sea, I am a mermaid, free, light and eternal. I love letting myself get lost in space as I travel through the sea. I feel the purity of nature much more intensely while I am away from the human chaos of the land. However, as globalization started to occur, I started to see the negative sides of "human progress" both on and off of land. While at sea, I encountered evils that made me question my optimistic outlook on human destiny and the future of the planet.

The first brutality I witnessed upon my return to the sea happened early one morning, while the full moon lit up the sky before the sun made its appearance. My emotions were already heightened, connected to the perplexing powers of the moon. However, the sight I was about to see was not something I would ever be able to emotionally prepare for. As I swam my way around jetting islands of rocky land and dreamy blue waters, I came upon a cove. I could hear the familiar sounds of dolphins communicating underwater, but I soon realized the dolphins I happened upon were trapped inside the cove. Before I could try to comprehend what was happening, a group of fishermen entered the bay in small boats. They quickly started to slaughter the dolphins one by one, turning the sea from a dreamy blue to a sinister red. I noticed that certain dolphins were spared their life. I wondered why particular dolphins were allowed to live, taken captive for some reason I couldn't quite imagine at the time. I would come to find that the young dolphins that weren't killed would be taken prisoner, sent to live out the rest of their days in aquariums, zoos or theme parks. These dolphins, taken captive for the mere amusement of humans, would be forced to perform and live each day in the tiny tanks that would now be "home," slaves to the humans. I started to weep as I thought about the unnecessary, selfish suffering humans inflict on each other as well as on so many other creatures of the earth.

I nervously wondered what would happen should a human capture me, *a mermaid*. I remembered the day I was caught in a net, a long time ago by Captain Drake and his crew. I remembered how scared I had been, trapped in the hands of people who had the potential to do whatever they wanted with me. I thought about what life would be like for me had I not been so kindly released by Francis. I shuddered at the thought of being put on display in a tank. Freedom is one of the most important things to me. Without the ability to go where I wanted and do what I wanted, I wondered if life would even be worth living. If the humans were to find out I was a mermaid, surely they would want to study me, or at the very least, put me on display as some strange form of entertainment. I became more and more fearful as I thought about what might happen if I were to get caught. I saw what humans had done to other creatures of the earth, enslaving, torturing and disrespecting beings of every kind. The last thing I wanted was to spend the remainder of my days locked up for someone's sick sense of amusement. I started to wonder, could it be possible I hadn't met any other mermaids because the humans killed them off? I had never met a species so destructive until I met the humans. Was it possible that a long time ago, humans killed off mermaids in some kind of holocaust? Or could it be that humans captured all the mermaids of the past to display in zoos and marine amusement parks, slowly killing the spirit (and eventually the flesh) that plays by freedom's side? Are there any more like me out there today? I angered as these thoughts crossed my mind. Though none of it likely occurred, it wouldn't be beyond the humans' capability.

I wish I could say the dolphin drive hunt was the only horrific act at sea I saw committed by the humans, but that wasn't the case. As I traveled through the ocean, there is no doubt I continued to see beauty, however, I also noticed much more pollution and much less life. I would be out on a remote island, far removed from any human activity, but I would still find garbage washing up on the pristine sands. It seemed the earth was sick, aging quicker as humans continued to contaminate it. Ecosystems were off balance and animals were scarcer as over-fishing and pollution made survival much more difficult. When did the earth become ill? Could humans be a part of the disease? Could they be a part of the cure?

Not too long after I witnessed the dolphin slaughter, I saw a number of other bloodcurdling acts committed by humans. I watched fishermen slaughtering sharks solely for their fins. As the popularity of shark fin soup grew, millions of sharks were slaughtered every year just for their fins. I watched fishermen cut off the fins (the most valuable part) of sharks and discard of the rest of the body, leaving the sharks to die painful, bloody deaths.

I also watched tuna fishermen follow pods of dolphins to easily catch the tuna. The fishermen would end up killing millions of not only dolphins, but also sharks and other fish as bycatch. I saw dolphins psychologically traumatized and babies left behind because they were unable to keep up as pods were chased. All of these sights made me sick and depressed. I felt hopeless and forlorn. One would think all this devastation would leave me numb, but it continued to anger and sadden me. I don't think anything could prepare me for the debacle I would see next. I was in a deep inlet of the Pacific Ocean, contemplating where I needed to go next. Should I enter the land again, or stay out at sea? A huge pod of orcas gracefully swam past me. Their beauty mesmerized me. The tight knit families were traveling through the vast ocean together, looking after one another. The ocean was their playground. I followed in their shadows, admiring how the mothers kept their babies close, drawn to the love I felt amongst these powerful and intelligent animals. I have tried to erase what I saw next from my memory so many times, but the cries I heard can never be eradicated from my mind. With the use of speed-boats, deafening explosives and airplanes, a group of men herded orcas into an enormous net. The orcas were frantically squealing and clicking, lifting themselves out of the water as they tried to get help from the family members outside of the net. As babies were taken from their mothers, I could see nothing but desperation and sorrow in both the mothers' and their young calves' eyes. I had witnessed the murder of a whale before, but these people were not killing the whales, rather they were capturing them. As the babies were forced into slings and pulled out of the ocean, I sensed these beautiful creatures would never know freedom again. I started to cry hysterically, wondering what was wrong with the world. The whales captured would be shipped off to aquariums and marine parks around the world, made to perform and eventually die in tiny cement pools, never to see their families again.

For whatever reason, I feel deeply connected to these creatures of the sea. I have an emotional attachment to them and a desire to protect them. These animals, so elegant and gentle, mean so much to me. It's a feeling that can hardly be described with words. After witnessing these whales taken captive, the last thing I wanted to do was enter a land where people so arrogantly believed they could do what they wanted with whatever they wanted. I was sad and disgusted by my recent experiences with the humans at sea, a space I once considered to be my refuge.

I decided to stay out at sea awhile longer to try to clear my mind and find some hope. Though I hit a low, life was still fascinating. I tried to find some sort of meaning in everything. Is there a purpose to the lives we all live? Or are we all just here for no reason at all?

As I came upon endless bodies of plastics and garbage, I questioned my previous beliefs that the earth was moving in the right direction. I had always thought ease of travel and communication across the world was a good thing, but I was seeing firsthand the destruction that came along with it. The earth couldn't sustain the way things were going. Because it takes hundreds of years for plastics to break down, virtually all the plastic ever created floats through the ocean, forming masses of garbage as big as countries. Every year, hundreds of thousands of sea birds and marine mammals are killed from plastics in the ocean. I went through a long period of depression as I watched sea turtles losing limbs as plastic rings cut into their skin and saw albatrosses swooping down to eat plastics they mistook for food.

Though I started to lose hope, I started to think back on all my experiences. I thought about all the inspirational humans I had met in all the centuries I had been wandering about the globe. I realized that while many humans are just here living day by day, trying to get by and survive in this crazy world, most had the right intentions. As I watched more beautiful sunrises and sunsets and contemplated the twinkling stars in the dark night sky, I found a light. Humans had created some unbelievable things. With progress comes set backs, however, I regained my faith in the human race as I thought about all the times humans had proven to me their want and ability to make the world a better place. I didn't know how long I had been at sea, but it had been enough. I was anxious to see what humans were up to now. Surely, the land was a new place since I had last stepped foot on it. Things were changing fast and I was ready to once again live life, as the humans were, curious as to what may have changed since my last land adventures. I knew not everything would be good on land, but I had a feeling big changes had occurred that would have shifted the life on land I once knew. I never could have dreamed of what I would find when I finally decided to trade in my fin for feet this time around.

THIRTY

THE INTERNET

Florida
2015

I washed ashore in Fort Lauderdale to find that life on land was definitely different than how I left it. One of the main reasons it was so different was because of something called The Internet. It was a hard concept for me to understand at first. How could you access any information online? How could you write someone a letter and send it via email, through the air? It was hard for me to grasp the fact that anyone could communicate across the world whenever they wanted. I was in awe that with access to the Internet one could obtain any information they could possibly want to know. What an exciting time it was!

As I spent more time on land, I realized that people now were much more aware and connected to things happening all around the world than they used to be. Because of the Internet, people were constantly being exposed to information. Nothing was as foreign as it used to be. Traveling was also much easier which added to the fact that the world seemed much smaller.

I mentioned earlier that in the 1930's, a flight from London to Brisbane, Australia would take 11 days with 12 stops in between. Now, you could be practically anywhere in the world in just a day! In South Florida, I noticed a blend of different people and cultures. It seemed the world was slowly becoming "one." People were more accepting and open to other cultures as people intermixed and intermingled.

It is funny because I have met a number of people who complain about the Internet and how it is ruining this generation. There are those who believe that the Internet is causing people to become addicted to the online world, losing their sense of reality and ability to make connections with actual human beings. Others have argued that people can find inappropriate and illegal material online or that criminals may use the Internet to spread viruses. While I can agree that these may be valid concerns, the Internet seemed to offer endless possibilities in aiding the world in its shift in the right direction.

There will always be the people who will abuse whatever it is that is in front of them. People may become addicted to the Internet, just as they would become addicted to anything else. Along with the good, there will always be bad. However, as I entered this new world, I was inspired by the changes occurring amongst the humans. I met people who were finally aware of the cruelties happening around the world. There were movements happening all over with the help of the Internet. People understood the planet was sick and people were working toward making things better. Injustices were brought to light much quicker with the Internet and people from all over the world could share thoughts and ideas instantly. As a whole, I felt as if the world was more connected than ever before.

Humans had the world in the palm of their hands. Anything they wanted to know could be found out with the click of a few buttons. For as long as I had been traveling the globe, I had never seen humans with so much power. It was incredible.

As I familiarized myself with the inventions that had become so commonly used in this new world, I got to thinking. I had experienced quite a bit in my life so far. I had always felt the need to record some of my thoughts and adventures in personal journals, however, maybe the world could benefit from some of the knowledge I had picked up along the way. Humans live such short existences here on Earth. It seemed my centuries of travel might be of value. I had seen much more than anyone living now, so why not put it out there? What better time to write a book than now, when people all across the world could have access to it? Plus, I would have the Internet to guide me while writing the book. I have never been good with dates since time is somewhat irrelevant to me, so I could use the Internet to help me piece together at what time period I was traveling through various locations. I could look up facts and statistics to give a broader perspective of what was happening at my times of travel, and I would surely expand my knowledge with all the research involved in writing about my travels through time and place on this amazing planet.

So here I was, in Fort Lauderdale, with nothing but my own personal experiences, the Internet, paper, a pen and all the time I could possibly want. I was ready to start writing.

THIRTY-ONE

WHAT I KNOW

A fter thousands of years of travel, I know that I still don't know. I don't have the answers to why we are here or what our existences mean. I don't have solutions to the many problems earth is currently facing and I don't know what the future holds. However, I have picked up on some things throughout my time traveling the vast lands of the planet. The time I spent with the creatures of the earth has taught me more than I ever could have imagined. While there is much I don't know, there are a few things I do know.

I have found that people are people. Over the course of thousands of years and from landmass to landmass, I have found that people resemble each other in personality and emotions. You will find greedy people, generous people, hateful people, loving people, closed-minded people, understanding people, curious people, kind people, and every other kind of person from generation to generation, wherever you go. And everyone seems to experience a variety of emotions from time to time. I am not exempt from these emotions. Animals are also not exempt from these emotions.

I have also found myself drawn to the family unit. As I have watched pods of dolphins swim alongside one another protecting and watching over each other, seen the unbreakable bond between a mother elephant and her precious baby, and spent time amongst human families who would do anything for one another, I felt the instinctual importance of family. Family is there, always. Family brings the feelings of protection and unconditional love. As a girl of the ocean, I have often felt envious of the other creatures on earth that seemed to have a parent as a teacher and a nurturer. However, I have also found that "family" does not have to be limited to the one you are born into. Some connections you form throughout your life are stronger than even the family bond. Those same connections hold true for creatures of all kinds. Just as I have formed unbreakable friendships with certain humans, I have had bonds with certain animals that were equally meaningful. There is no limit to or explanation for the connections we form.

I believe we are here on earth for a reason. I can't tell you what that reason is, but I truly feel as if we are part of something so much bigger. While I think we all have a purpose, I think at the very least, we are here to enjoy. There is so much beauty to be appreciated. If you do nothing else with your life, have fun, taste the sweet fruits that grow from the land, feel the warm sun on your skin, listen to music that makes your feet move and your mind spin, smell the lovely scents of flowers wafting through the air, watch the divine sunrises and sunsets, do things that ignite the passion in your soul and surround yourself with as much love as possible. Don't try to hold on to anything because everything is bound to change. Beauty is fleeting but forever returning. Listen, learn and appreciate everything this earth has to offer.

As the earth continues to shift and change, realize you are a part of all that is happening. Everything is connected in one way or another. I feel that the earth is moving toward something. I think that "something" is good.

Everything has a unique purpose. Follow your path and listen to your intuition. Just as birds know to fly south for the winter, sea turtles know to faithfully return to the same beach each time they are ready to nest, and spiders know how to weave their intricate webs, you were born knowing what to do as well. It is easy to let other people's paths cloud yours, but try to tune in to that individual calling you were born with. To the person reading this now: if this is hitting you in a strangely personal way, it means something. You are here to do something. You know what to do.

THIRTY-TWO

NOW

_____

ere I am now, with you, living on this planet. Now is the time. It is the time to question the normalcies of our current societies, it is the time to work towards healing the planet, it is the time to open our minds and unite, and it is the time to dig deep down into our personal consciences to figure out our unique purposes.

As the general consciousness shifts, great changes will occur. These changes are already happening as more and more people realize we have the potential to save the planet. Humans hold the power to create a heaven here on earth. It is all a matter of forgetting what we're told and tapping into and listening to the intelligence of the Universe.

While there are still so many injustices happening every day and the world often seems hopeless as people wrong each other and destroy the planet we all call home, the only thing you can do is rise above. People have the power to change the world. Don't let the people who entangle themselves in the web of societal fallacies bring you down. Now is the time to do what you feel to be right. Don't try too hard. Just do what you feel and the rest will follow. You may not know what the future holds but you've got to learn to trust. I think that is one of the biggest lessons I have learned in my life. Trusting is of utmost importance. The lives we all live are crazy, unique, and often unnerving. But once you learn to trust, everything falls into place. Trust in the kindness of others, trust in your own intuition, and trust in the Universe.

Realize your actions, even in the simplest of ways, affect everything. The way you live your life is the way you change the world. If you live with love, it will illuminate the world around you. Every little thing you say, the thoughts in your head, how you put your body to work and the dreams you imagine, all shape "reality." You may not realize it, but everything you do changes the world. Everything you put out there, in both thoughts and actions, floats through the air and swims through the sea, mixing with the thoughts and actions of all the other beings on this earth. Spend time alone, form your own personal thoughts and experiences and then figure out what you are here to do. Once you figure out what you need to do *now*, you will always know what to do as the future creeps in.

As I sit here now, concluding my book of adventures, life lessons, and wonderments, I feel as alive as ever. I don't know what will happen next, but I am excited for whatever life holds. I know I will continue to change. The beings I cross paths with will further change me, the sights I continue to see will change me, and my necessary times of solitude will change me. And I know I will persist in changing the world. As I continue to ride the chaotic wave of life, I know there is nothing to fear. Heaven is here.

ABOUT THE AUTHOR

Alanna Murphy is a young, enthusiastic writer with a degree in Communications from The University of Florida. She has traveled extensively and believes traveling is the best way to not only learn about the world but to also learn about oneself. Aside from her interests in writing and traveling, Alanna is also an artist. All the sketches included in this novel are Alanna's creations.

CPSIA information can be obtained
at www.ICGtesting.com
Printed in the USA
BVHW07s1824010718
520505BV00003B/16/P